PRAISE FOR "WOOM"

"This is grimy, gritty and nasty stuff. But it is done with wit and literary flair. *Woom* is the work of talent. An absolute masterpiece. I don't use those words lightly."
J.R. Park, Author of *Upon Waking*

"*Woom* is a novel that achieves a lot in a very short amount of time. It's complex and surprising from start to finish. It's also truly horrifying - but in the best way possible."
Adiba Jaigirdar, Cultured Vultures

"Blends the cynicism of Chuck Palahniuk, the greasy and believable characterisation of Irvine Welsh, and the vivid ghastliness of the more literary examples of pulp horror, in order to create a multi-layered tale that keeps its cards close to its chest right up to its abhorrent finale."
Jonathan Butcher, The Ginger Nuts of Horror

"An excellent example of some of the exciting dark fiction being written today and a tale that will leave a lasting impression on any horror fan brave enough to read it."
Adrian Shotbolt, Beavis the Bookhead

"Three days after finishing the final word I still couldn't bring myself to even crack open the cover of something new. Not because I didn't enjoy *Woom*, but due to the power and strength living inside the writing."
Alex Kimmell, Confessions of a Reviewer

Shadow Work Publishing

www.ShadowWorkPublishing.com

ISBN-13: 978-0995242340
ISBN-10: 0995242348

www.DuncanRalston.com

WOOM

An Extreme Horror Novel

Duncan Ralston

2nd Printing, Shadow Work Publishing

CONTENT(S)

ROOM 6

ANGEL OPENED THE door to Room 6 with a key so scratched he was surprised it still worked, linked to a vermillion fob worn by so many thumbs the number was barely visible. The old room was just as he remembered it—this was not a good thing. There was no nostalgia here for Angel, only pain. Some places hold the pain in their walls, in the carpet snags, in the cracks of the ceiling and chinks in the baseboards. Room 6 of the Lonely Motel thirty minutes from the New York-Canadian border was one such place, Angel believed. With quiet apprehension, he hoisted the heavy black backpack onto his shoulder and crossed the threshold.

"Hello, Mom," he said to the empty room. "It's been a long time."

Angel dropped the bag on a threadbare carpet the same shade as the key fob, and gave the room a careful examination. The flowery bedspread was new—he supposed it made sense, considering. The solid wood bed-frame, and possibly the mattress if they'd been able to get the red out, were still the same.

The painting stuck to the wood paneling above

was the same: a poor oil rendition of Jonah escaping the whale. The same faux red oak dresser and vanity, chipped in the lower right corner, warped near the top like a carnival mirror, so if you stood on your tiptoes your head would stretch out long and pointy. The ashtray was new, a cheap black plastic one. The last time he'd been here, the front desk had requested no smoking, though they'd smoked anyway. You had to, just to get rid of the smell.

Angel sat on the bed and kicked off his shoes. He lay back on the pillows (too large and firm—he preferred thin and soft, though it didn't matter as he wouldn't be sleeping), and drew his knees up to his chest. He remained in that position for several minutes, reflecting on the memory of pain while staring at the closet and bathroom doors, one closed, the other open. Cigarettes and cheap perfume lingered alongside the musty stink of the carpet and the eye-watering dryer sheet smell of the bedspread.

Pain.

Angel knew a lot about pain. *Too* much. With any luck, his pain would end today. He would turn the clock back. He would start fresh.

This room was where it all started, he thought. *Fitting that it should end here, too.*

Struck by sudden nausea, Angel got up and staggered to the bathroom. He raised the toilet seat hastily, managing to drop to his knees before a deluge of undigested breakfast burrito and sour mash whisky poured out of him into the bowl, splashing on the rim and the back of the lid. He coughed several times and spat a thick wad of brown saliva into the mess of frothy puke, much of it floating on the surface, before flushing twice to wash away the last straggling chunks of vomit, and rising slowly to his feet.

The same mirror as before reflected his haggard face. Shaved bald, his tan dome glistened under the too-bright bulb above the mirror. The bags under his eyes were nearly as heavy and dark as the backpack he'd brought with him.

Angel had always been uncomfortably aware of what most people would consider his "ugly" features. A long, jagged scar ran up the left side of his face, and his head tapered on top like an egg, a feature that had only become noticeable once he'd shaved it. Although not technically a "pinhead," he'd been called it several times by those lower on the evolutionary chain than himself. Dressing well seemed to direct attention away from said features, which was why he wore a crisp pencil stripe Armani dress shirt, black wool pants with a sharp pleat (Hugo Boss), and red silk socks by Paul Smith. The shoes beside the bed were Gucci brown leather, polished so their shine matched that of his head.

Angel flicked off the bathroom light and gave the tub a passing glance before leaving. He sat down on the edge of the bed, and reached for the phone on the bedside table, the same old black rotary phone he'd called 911 from the second-last time he'd been here, on his way out the door. He picked up the clunky receiver and began to dial.

"Yes, hello. I'd like a girl." He paused, listening to the dispatcher. "She has to be heavyset. That's right, the larger the better. Now, the last time I sent for someone the girl wasn't what I'd ordered, so I'm going to say it again: *large* woman. Attractiveness unimportant. Okay?" He listened. Her dry, nasally apology irritated him, but he kept his anger in check. "China? *Shyla*. She sounds perfect. I'm at the Lonely Motel, Room 6. Yes, the one near the airport. Thank you."

Hanging up the phone, Angel hoped they'd get it right. His whole day depended on it. He lay back and waited, thinking again about pain.

ANGEL WOKE TO a delicate rap on the door. The bedside clock showed he'd been out for an hour. His sticky mouth tasted like a dog's asshole. He'd fallen asleep on top of the blanket in the fetal position, and his knees were stiff. Standing painfully, he shook out his legs before crossing to the door. He squinted through the peephole at the woman he'd ordered. Either the escort agency had gotten it right this time, or the peephole was giving him a more narrow view than normal. She appeared to be out of breath from climbing the stairs, which bode well.

Anxiously, Angel opened the door.

Shyla stood there in all her fleshy glory, sun-pinked shoulders exposed, the rest of her upper body draped in a black silk shawl and a gold lamé mini dress (which actually was quite *maxi* considering her size). Her freckled legs were bare, her chubby little toes—painted cherry red—peeking out from strappy platform shoes. Her chestnut hair with blonde highlights was wrapped and coiled on her head like a cinnamon roll.

"Hi there. I'm Angel. You must be Shyla."

He stuck out a hand, and she shook it delicately in her own, her expression making it obvious previous clients hadn't gotten her accustomed to social graces.

"Please," he said, "come in."

The escort smiled, and stepped inside. "Such a gentleman," she said, her voice high and throaty. He imagined she'd do well working for a phone sex hotline, but he also suspected she brought in enough cash in her current vocation. The acronym BBW—Big Beautiful Woman—had taken up much of the back pages of the paper where he'd originally found the agency's number. Hers seemed to be the biggest niche alongside "she-male" and Asian.

"Wasn't this motel closed for health violations?"

"You know, I think it was," he said as he closed the door behind them and drew the chain lock.

"I don't mean to be rude," she said, turning back to face him with an undisguised sneer, "but this place is a shit-hole."

"I don't disagree."

He stepped past her, breathing in her sweet

perfume and a slight tang of sweat, as she reached into her Chanel clutch purse and took out a pack of cigarettes.

"You mind if I smoke?"

"Be my guest."

He turned the chair in front of the dresser to face the bed, and sat while Shyla lit a long, thin cigarette. She blew a puff of smoke into the wide shaft of sunlight from between the curtains, holding eye contact with him. The not-unpleasant smell of mentholated tobacco filled the air between them.

"Is that your real name? Angel?"

"Is Shyla yours?"

Chuckling dryly, she exhaled a thick cloud. "Touché."

"You can sit on the bed, if you like."

She eyed it with distaste.

"It's clean. Really, it is. I just slept on it for an hour or so."

"It kind of smells like puke."

"I think the maid did a bad job cleaning the toilet," Angel said.

"That's a lovely thought, isn't it?"

Hesitantly, Shyla sat down on the bed. The springs squeaked as she sank into the mattress. Flesh hung from every part of her, Angel saw. Her large, swaying hips, her arms, her buttocks—even her eyelids were heavy. He examined her body with clinical detachment: a gynecologist's gaze. He was neither aroused, nor repulsed. She was merely a vessel. A *thing* to be filled and then discarded.

"So," she said, raising her eyebrows suggestively. "Why don't you come a little closer, cutiepie?"

Angel crossed his arms. "I'm fine here for now."

The woman blew a smoke ring and shrugged. "If you wanna waste your money talking, that's up to you."

He admired her directness, though aside from the few Asian women the agency had sent, all of the escorts he'd ordered had tended to be blunt. "Oh, we'll get down to business soon," he assured her. "I just want to ask you a few questions first. The more questions you answer, the bigger the tip."

"I hope that isn't the only big thing you got for me," she said, gazing at his crotch with a smirk.

"Are you a size queen, Shyla?"

Her boisterous laughter made him grin in spite of himself. "That's funny. You're a funny guy, Angel. What, are you writing an article? A little exposé about sex workers for HuffPo or something?"

"I'm not a writer. I do have some stories to tell, but those will come later."

"I hope they're aren't the only things that *come*," Shyla winked, and when Angel's mouth became very small from annoyance, she said, "Sure, I'll answer your questions. Go ahead."

"Do you have children, Shyla?"

She blew out smoke on a surprised laugh. "Not that it's any of your business, but no."

He studied her face long enough that she

widened her eyes challengingly, taking another long drag of her cigarette.

"Thank you for being honest," he said. "Have you ever thought of having children?"

"What woman hasn't?"

"You speak for your whole gender, do you?"

"Yes, then," she said with a tone of aggravation.

"Why haven't you?"

Her eyes narrowed. "Next question."

"Fair enough." Angel thought carefully about how to phrase the question in a way that wouldn't sound crazy. He didn't want to spook her now that he had her in the room. But since she'd been direct with him, he decided to do likewise. "Do you believe in ghosts?" he asked.

Her chin wobbled with laughter. "You really are funny, you know that?"

"I'm serious. *Do* you?"

"Is this one of those hidden camera pranks?" She stubbed out her cigarette in a flurry of sparks. "Seriously, is this a joke? Because it's not funny if it is."

"My mother died in this room," Angel told her, not wanting to admit to it, only saying it so she'd calm down. But the relief of it, letting go of that secret after holding it inside for so long, washed over him like a tsunami. The pain lessened. He reached out to the woman on the bed. "May I have a cigarette?"

Her hard look had softened. "Sure you can, sweetie."

As she handed him the pack of Virginia Slim 120's, her long, glossy white acrylic nails grazed his fingers. He plucked a smoke from the pack, his hand shaking badly, and nestled it between his lips. Shyla flicked her Zippo and held the flame under the tip as he dragged on it. He'd quit smoking years ago, only indulging in a puff here and there. Usually the first one felt like razors in his throat, but the menthol and lightness of the tobacco made it feel like he was breathing in minty dust. The nicotine calmed him immediately.

"Honestly?" she said. "I saw a ghost once. So yes, I do believe in ghosts. Do you?"

"I'm not sure. I believe pain lingers. Do I believe in spirits? In the supernatural? Probably not."

She nodded. "Do you mind if I take off my shoes?"

Angel raised a foot, wiggling his toes under the sock. "Make yourself comfortable."

Shyla hunched over her belly with a groan, and lifted her right foot with surprising flexibility. He supposed being limber would be a benefit to her profession. She undid the straps, placed the shoe on the floor, and did the same for the left foot. "That's better," she said with a sigh, squeezing her arches.

"That's a nice color," Angel remarked.

She smiled down at her red toenails. "You like 'em?"

"Yeah, it, uh... it matches the carpet."

Shyla peered down at the carpet, then at the window. "It's called 'Vermillion Dollar Baby.' It also matches the drapes," she added with a sly grin—though considering her hair color, he doubted the statement's veracity. When he didn't take the bait, she said, "Is that all? No more questions?"

"I have one more. This one is more... metaphorical in nature."

"Shoot," she said, tugging out another cigarette. Angel handed his to her. She eyed it cautiously.

"It's okay, I don't have a disease."

Shyla took it and put it in her mouth. "You fish-lipped it."

Angel apologized.

"I've had worse things in my mouth." Shyla shrugged and ran her silver tongue ring over her bottom teeth—*clack clack clack*, like a can rattling on prison bars. The gesture was meant to be seductive. In conjunction with what she'd said, Angel felt only mild repugnance.

"Do you think... places... absorb bad things?"

"What do you mean 'bad things'?"

"Like betrayal. Anger. *Death*. When you first walked in here, how did it make you feel?"

"I felt... disgusting, honestly. Evil. Like I shouldn't touch anything or it might infect me. Now that I've been in here for a bit it's not as bad as it was. It's kind of quaint, honestly." She looked up at the frame above the bed. "That painting's got to go, though."

"It's awful, isn't it?"

Shyla raised her eyebrows in agreement. "Is that

Moby Dick?"

"Jonah and the Whale. Do you know the story?"

Nodding, she said, "The nuns gave us the CliffsNotes version in Sunday school." She seemed to catch something in his look, because she added, "That's right, the prostitute was a good little Catholic schoolgirl."

"So you know God made the whale eat Jonah because Jonah had turned away from Him. You know he lived inside the belly of the whale for three days and three nights, until he gave in and prayed to God, who commanded the whale puke him out."

"That's not a fat joke, is it?"

"I'm just telling a story."

She looked at him until she appeared to be satisfied he wasn't making fun of her, then she nodded. "Well, good then. Because I'll do a lot of things for money, but I won't stand for that. I'm no carnival freak."

"Do I strike you as someone who has any right to make fun of the way someone looks?"

She shrugged. "I dunno. I like bald guys. And that scar makes you look like a James Bond villain, which is kind of hot, to be honest."

Angel laughed.

"What can I say?" the prostitute said. "I like bad boys."

He smiled patiently. "Back to my original point," he said, "I don't believe in ghosts. But I do think places, like this motel room, I think they hold on to bad things, the way people hold on to memories. Grief. Pain. Disease. Addiction. I think when you enter a place that's absorbed enough bad things, it pukes them out at you. It *drenches* you in them. So a relatively innocuous room, like this one, will appear evil. Because *bad things happened here*."

"Like your mother."

"Like my mother," he nodded. "Like other things. Do you think the whale missed Jonah, when he was gone?"

Shyla snorted laughter. "What?"

He tried a different tack. "Do you ever think about luggage?"

"Luggage?"

"Bags. Suitcases. Backpacks, like this one," he said, tapping the bag he'd brought with a socked toe.

"I know what luggage is. Is this another metaphor?"

Angel ignored her, trying not to lose his train of thought. "When something… carries… something else, for a long period of time, do you think it remembers it? Do you think it's possible it absorbs a part of it, on an atomic level?"

"That's a really weird question."

"I'm a weird person."

Shyla nodded. "This is definitely the strangest date I ever had. And I've been with guys who get off shitting in diapers and begging for a spanking."

Angel raised an eyebrow in curiosity.

"Honestly," she said, laughing. "You wouldn't

believe the kind of things some of these guys want to get into. I guess it's because I'm a heavy woman, it makes them feel smaller. They want me to mother them. Suck on my tits, burp them, that kind of thing."

"I'm not interested in diapers, Shyla. But that wouldn't be the craziest thing that's happened in this room. Not by a longshot."

"Oh yeah? Well, like what? Give me an example."

"Okay." He took in a deep breath. "I'll tell you one, but I have to warn you, it's pretty grim."

"Worse than a grown man shitting diapers and calling me 'Mommy'?"

"I think so."

"Huh. Well, okay. Let's hear it."

"Just let me decide where to begin."

He didn't need time, it was part of the game. He'd told the story so many times he could recite it in his sleep. And so he began, like he always did, with: "See, there was this kid named Johnny, and—"

CRAM(PS)

JOHNNY LOVED JENNY, even though they'd only been dating for a few months, and he thought she loved him back. He'd only ever loved one other girl in his life and it had ended badly, so when he met Jenny he decided he would do anything for her. Whatever she asked, there'd always be this little twinkle in her eyes, and he would do it. She was high on life, and Johnny couldn't resist.

"Let's go bungie jumping!"

"Okay."

"Let's go to Vegas!"

"Okay."

"Let's try heroin!"

Obviously, saying *yes* all the time had begun to become a problem.

Johnny didn't take to heroin. They smoked it, since neither of them could stand the thought of using a needle, and he puked his guts out. After that he was sweaty and shaky for half the day, like a bad fever. No good effects whatsoever. He was already addicted to oxy from a previous injury, so he thought maybe that was the reason it didn't work for him.

Jenny though, she had this look in her eyes like

she got when she was riding him cowgirl and close to cumming. Eyes rolled back in her head, eyelashes fluttering. All curled up on the bed like a baby, knees up to her chest, she stuck her thumb in her mouth and just laid that way for hours while Johnny puked and shivered on the bathroom floor.

When he came around, she was making breakfast. "Let's do it again," she said, but that twinkle in her eye was gone, and she ate the eggs she'd scrambled straight out of the pan off the wooden spoon.

Johnny didn't want to, but he said *okay* because that was the pattern. Wash, rinse, repeat.

The next day when Johnny came home from work, Jenny had already dipped into the heroin, and she was curled up on the bed again with her thumb in her mouth like the day before. Burning eggs smoldered in a pan on the stove and their lower flat had filled with smoke. If he hadn't got home when he did, Jenny probably would have died from smoke inhalation, which in retrospect would have spared her and Johnny a lot of pain, but he'd been let off work earlier than normal, and he ran around madly opening up all the windows before using the door like a fan, swinging it open and closed to try and clear the smoke faster.

When he could breathe a bit better, he went back to check on Jenny, and she seemed to be breathing fine. Shallow, but she looked okay. The needle she'd used, the lighter and the spoon, blackened on the underside and little purple-brown bubbles encrusted in the bowl, all of this was spread out on the bedside table. The little baggie still had a fair amount of brown powder in it, but Johnny had no real urge to taste it or smoke it and especially not to use the needle like Jenny had because he was still coasting on his last few oxys—and anyway, who the hell would want to do a drug that made you so unaware you'd let your scrambled eggs burn down to a pile of black ash while you zoned out on the bed with your thumb stuck in your mouth like a baby? It seemed reckless, and Johnny decided he would tell her so as soon as she was sober.

They argued for hours before Johnny gave in. Jenny made it seem like he was the problem for not wanting to join her, even though she hadn't waited for him to come home before shooting up, and by the end of the night Johnny was so tired of arguing he could almost see her point.

The next day, he came home to the same sight: Jenny curled up on the bed, thumb jammed in her mouth. The next day, the same. Wash, rinse, repeat. *At least the house isn't on fire*, he kept thinking when he walked in the door every night. She didn't even eat anymore, just the occasional dry piece of toast and saltines.

One day about a month into this routine, Johnny came home to find a skinny little white guy sitting on his bed alongside Jenny. The way they were looking at him, it was pretty obvious they'd just been talking about him as he came through the door. Johnny was suspicious, naturally, coming home to find another man on their bed, and since the two of them hadn't fooled around since she started shooting up, he assumed the two must be fucking, even though both of them were clothed and sitting a few feet apart.

"This is Juicy," Jenny told him.

"Pleasure to make your acquaintance," Juicy said, sticking out a hand that may or may not have just been finger-blasting Johnny's girlfriend. He wasn't about to shake hands with some stranger sitting on his bed, either way. By then he'd had about enough of Jenny's shit, and this new development was just icing on the urinal cake.

Snubbed, Juicy shifted on the mattress, working out the kinks in his shoulders and rolling his head around like he'd just left the chiropractor's. "Oh, it's gon' be like that, is it?" he said, and Johnny said, "Tell me why the fuck you're sitting on my bed beside my girlfriend, and then maybe I'll shake your hand."

Jenny said his name like he'd just stepped in shit, and that's when Johnny knew for certain he was the only one getting fucked here. He had a bad feeling he was about to take it without lube.

"Let me lay it out for you," Juicy said. "Your girl here owes me money. A lot of it. And I'm not the type to let a debt go unpaid for too long."

"How much?" Johnny asked him, even though he didn't want to know the answer. He felt like the time they'd gone bungie jumping, the earth dropping out from under his feet and his heart in his throat.

"Six large."

"How much is that?" Johnny asked Jenny.

Jenny told him it was six thousand dollars, giving him this look like *I dare you to start with me*, and if Juicy hadn't been there he might have. Instead he said, "We don't have that kind of money."

"That's where you're in luck," Juicy said. "I was just elucidating to your girl Jenny, if she sees fit to help me in my current predicament, I might could consider letting that debt slide. Shit, I might even be obliged to send a little good luck her way, you know'm sayin'?"

Johnny had no idea what Juicy was saying, so the man laid it all out for him, the way he'd apparently laid it all out for Jenny, who kept nodding her head at all the parts she remembered in her post-heroin zombie state.

Juicy and his supplier needed to get a large shipment of heroin into Canada. Since border security had been tightened because of terrorism — this was around the time they caught the Toronto 18, back in 2006 — Juicy needed a mule to carry the drugs on a flight. The last couple of truck shipments got busted, he said, and they'd lost about fifty grand total. Juicy didn't want to lose any more money. That was where Jenny and Johnny came in.

"With mules," Juicy said, "you got your swallowers, and you got your stuffers. Obviously, swallowers swallow these wee little baggies or pellets filled with H or Molly or Tina, and stuffers, well they cram them thangs into whatever hole they can."

"So you want to use my girlfriend as human luggage," Johnny said.

Jenny shook her head. "You know me," she said. "I can't even swallow a vitamin without choking."

"Shoot, bitch just straight up admitted she don't deep throat!" Juicy said, giggling like a kid in sex ed.

"I'm not fucking muling heroin," Johnny said. "I've got a job. I've got a reputation to protect."

"So do I," Juicy said, sucking his teeth. "Cram 'em, swallow 'em, I don't give a fuck," Juicy said, with his cold-as-ice look. "You gotta man up and handle yo bidness. Your girl here, she look like kaka—no offense."

Jenny shrugged it off, but if it'd come from Johnny she likely would've slapped him.

"She look like an addict," Juicy said. "But you, even though it look like you got a little coffee in yo' cream, you look like a typical bidnessman. Look at that skinny-ass tie. What is that, Hugo Boss or some shit? I put dis bitch on a flight, lookin' like she do, they be searchin' cavities she don't even know she *has* before she even get to security. Dude like you could walk onto a plane wearing a bomb shoutin' about how you wearing a bomb, and nobody would fuckin' blink."

Johnny sat down at the table, all the fight kicked out of him. "This is crazy," he said. "How the fuck am

I the one who ends up getting fucked here? This is fucking insane. Can't you see how insane this is?" he asks them, but of course they looked at him like he was the crazy one, and he's outnumbered.

So like usual, Johnny gives in.

Juicy starts rubbing his hands together excitedly, making a dry sound like a brush on a chalkboard. "That's real good," he said. "But if you mess with me, nigga, I'll find out where yo mama live and kill the fuck outta her."

"That won't be a problem," Johnny said.

A couple days later, they met at a motel room, *this* motel room, Room 6 at The Lonely. It was Juicy's choice of where to meet, and Johnny pondered fate and choices and how sometimes things just seemed to shift into place like a planetary alignment or a slot machine jackpot—not that he felt especially lucky. That was how he found himself in the cramped little bathroom back there, swallowing tiny pale peach egg-shaped baggies filled with black tar heroin, his tongue tasting like latex and baby powder.

"I can't swallow many more of these," Johnny groaned, literally gagging on the last one. His insides grumbled as if to back up his complaint, but he knew it was already too late to renege. At that point his only choices were to swallow the rest of them or shove them up his ass, and since his yearly proctology exams felt like a reenactment of the Battle of the Bulge, he supposed he'd just have to keep swallowing, pretty much like he'd kept swallowing

Jenny's shit ever since she'd started shooting *this* shit in her veins.

Sitting on the sink, Jenny urged him on with a halfhearted, "You can do it, baby," and rubbed his back like he was a toddler going potty his first time. She looked at the small clutch of baggies beside her on the counter. "It's just like twelve more bags," she said. "Maybe ten."

Just those "like twelve or ten bags" could feed her habit for a month or more, Johnny knew. Add that to the eighty or so he'd already swallowed—which felt more like a million—and she could live the high life for a year; two years or more if they went behind Juicy's back and sold it on the street themselves. The street value was more than fifty grand, according to Juicy, but since they had no connections here or in Canada, the chances of being able to unload it without getting busted or killed was slim to none.

Johnny put another small rubbery finger condom in his mouth, tied at the end, and swallowed it with a big gulp of water. The bag lodged in his throat, and he had to take another hard gulp to ease it down. His stomach was so stretched he could feel it settle among the others. His guts were like a piñata, if that piñata happened to be on the verge of butt-birthing a Chihuahua.

Jenny refilled the glass, and handed him another bag.

The cramps began violently in his lower intestines, though they moved like a bolt of lightning all the way up to his esophagus as he tried to swallow. Already sitting on the toilet (with the lid down), he knew it would be easy to drop his pants and purge himself of this painful demon, but Jenny would be disappointed, and Juicy would probably do the both of them. He'd held in a shit before. Who hadn't? He just had to grin through the pain. Trouble was, he'd have to hold it in for several hours. From the motel to the airport, throughout the flight to Canada, and again through customs. Six, seven hours, depending on the line and delays. He thought he'd be lucky to hold it in an hour at the most.

"Just two, three more, baby," Jenny told him, holding another baggie out. He'd heard somewhere you could overdose on water. Considering the bags of heroin in his guts, each one of them a potential time bomb, he supposed it should be the least of his worries.

"Come on, you can do this..."

Johnny shook his head, the last handful of baggies rising on his gorge. It was puke or shit or both now. The antacids hadn't helped, and the antidiarrheal — this package was about to be delivered whether he wanted to or not.

He bolted up from the toilet, doubled over in pain, and raised the lid, jerking down his jeans just in time to slap his bare ass cheeks on the seat.

Before Jenny could finish saying "Goddammit, Johnny, don't you fucking do it!" the baggies oozed out of him in a torrent of vile, smelly black shit, popping out of him like a wet string of anal beads, like .50 caliber ammunition complete with explosions—

"AW, COME ON, Angel..." Shyla said, visibly disgusted.

"Too much?"

"It's a little over the top, don't you think?"

"You've never had diarrhea before?"

"I don't poop," Shyla asserted, with a look of such sincerity Angel might have believed the Lord worked through her digestive system via Immaculate Defecation.

"If you can't hear about poop, the rest of the story isn't going to make a lot of sense. Just think of it like chocolate ice cream."

Sneering, Shyla said, "Don't ruin ice cream for me, too."

"You want me to stop?"

"Well, I kind of want to find out what happens..."

"Okay. Then back to the poo."

She sighed heavily, her freckled bosom rising and falling. "Fine, just... no more talking about the smell, okay? It makes me imagine it, and I don't want to imagine it any more than I already am."

"I'll abstain. If you promise no more interruptions."

"Cross my heart and hope to die," Shyla said, making the gesture.

* * *

"DON'T FLUSH THAT, or I'll fucking kill you myself!" Jenny yelled through the door as she slammed it behind her, proving what Johnny had known for several weeks: she loved the heroin more than she'd ever loved him, if she had at all.

The pressure on his bowels had lessened, but now his ass felt like he'd been fucked by a splintered dildo. Sweat glistened on his brow as he reached for the toilet paper and daubed his volcanic anus. He knew it wasn't possible he could have pooped all the baggies out in one go, but it had come out so violently he wouldn't doubt it if an x-ray revealed it to be true.

No matter how many baggies were in that toilet, all of them needed to come out. He wondered if the bags would float and remain in the toilet if he flushed, or if it would just overflow and create an even messier problem, but he knew he was just grasping at straws and time was running short. The flight was in two hours. He pulled up his pants, the cramps still rumbling through his insides, and searched the cupboard below the sink. A solitary toilet scrubber, flecked with dried brown matter, and a container of Comet powder met his disapproving gaze. No gloves.

He called out to Jenny to come help, but she refused. Didn't surprise him. She wouldn't even use the bathroom after him most times, and this time was far worse than any plague he'd unleashed on their own toilet at home.

So like a kid diving into a cold lake after the thaw,

he plugged his nose and plunged his hand into the soupy bowl to feel around for the bags. His fingers caught one immediately, and he pulled it out, dripping gobs of wet filth on the rim of the bowl and the floor tiles. *Plop* — into the sink. Back into the bowl. Feel around. Grab a handful this time, no point making more trips than absolutely necessary, *drip drip drip* on the tile and the counter and *plop* into the sink. Up to the middle of his forearm with goopy black particles, but still he plunged in again, to his elbow this time, reaching deep into the bowl where it started to bend, and when he was done what felt like an eternity later, all told there were twenty-seven bags in the sink waiting to be cleaned and swallowed again.

Wash, rinse, repeat. Wash, rinse, repeat. That was his mantra now.

Flushing the toilet, the color of his stool troubled him, but he assumed it was something to do with the concoction of stomach pills he'd taken to keep the baggies down. If it was heroin in his system he knew he'd be dead already, a realization that came as cold comfort.

Curious, he peered into the bowl. A torn baggie floated on top, like a spent condom. He supposed it must have split on a fingernail when he was swamp fishing since he didn't feel at all high — even the oxys had worn off at this point — and he figured Juicy wouldn't quibble about one bag when there were still close to a hundred undamaged baggies left inside him.

"Is it done yet?" Jenny shouted at the door. He could hear the TV on in the room, one of her goddamn reality shows, a bunch of women yelling at each other for God knew what reason.

"It's done," he said. "But I can't swallow these bags. I'm sick. I'm holding these ones in by the skin of my teeth. Just get in here, okay?"

He heard her exasperated sigh. A minute later the door opened, and she groaned, wafting away the lingering odor. "*Jesus*, Johnny, what the fuck?"

"I dunno, it must be the pills. Something didn't sit right."

"Well, you gotta get 'em back in there. Flight's in two hours."

"You think I don't know that? If I could swallow them I would, but they're just gonna come right back out again. You got us into this fucking mess," he said, "you have to step up."

"Step up? You *know* I can't swallow them—"

"Then cram them up your twat for all I care!"

She slapped him then. Hard.

"Look, you fucking do your share, or I'm walking," Johnny said, feeling good about standing up to her for once. It was like the bungie jumping, he was terrified walking up to the edge but once he jumped, it was all or nothing. "I've got nothing to lose."

"He'll kill us, Johnny."

"It's been a slice so far," Johnny said. "Maybe

we're better off."

Suddenly Jenny was all sweet and nice again. She nestled up close to him, running her fingers on the back of his neck. "You don't mean that," she said. "C'mon, Johnny, we had some fun."

The fun was so long ago with so much disappointment in between he could barely remember their trip to Vegas, the bungie jumping, those first few dates getting to know each other, their first tentative kiss, and their giggling fumbles to get each other's clothes off in the dark of her bedroom that first time. He pushed her away coldly.

"You need to handle your business," he said, and the look on her face told the story of their relationship in the span of three seconds. She hauled back and punched him in the chest. Once, twice, three times he let her. When she tried to hit him a fourth time, he grabbed her fist and held it down.

"The more you hit me, the more likely I am to shit the rest of these baggies into my pants," he said. "So go lie down on the bed and take off your jeans."

"What? You think I'm gonna let you rub up against me after all this? I *hate* you!"

"I hate you, too," Johnny said, as sincere as he'd ever been. "But right now we're a matching set of human luggage, and you need to get packing."

Her face went pale. "What—?" she said, so disgusted she couldn't even finish the thought.

"You heard what Juicy said. There are swallowers, and there are stuffers. You've stuffed *me* for the last time."

"I don't even have a ticket…" She was sullen, like a little girl who'd had her pigtails pulled in the playground one too many times.

"We'll get you a standby," Johnny said, and he nodded toward the bed. "Time's a-wasting."

Jenny shouldered past him into the room. She sat on the bed with an angry huff, and started to unbuckle her jeans. She pulled them down to her shins before taking off her runners, a weird habit that reminded Johnny of the first time they fooled around, her hopping around trying to get her heels off with her jeans already around her ankles.

She pulled her panties down past her skinned knees, and stood there in nothing but a T-shirt and her socks. She hadn't shaved in the weeks since they'd stopped fooling around, and her dark bush was a stark contrast to her chalk-white skin and straggly blonde hair. Jenny stood there for a second, as if awaiting his next command, so Johnny said, "Go ahead and lay down."

"You're an asshole, Johnny," she said. "When this is over—"

"I never want to see you again," he finished for her. "Good to see we're on the same page."

Jenny laid back against the bed with her knees together. He came back with his hands full of baggies, and he set them down between her socked feet.

"You want me to do it, or…?"

"You *wish*. You're never gonna touch my pussy again," Jenny said, her eyes darker than he'd ever seen them. But that twinkle was back, he noticed. Too little too late.

Jenny plucked up the first of the baggies, hesitating with it held near her pink slit. She told him to turn around, she couldn't do it with him watching. Johnny did as he was told, but he promised himself it was the last time he'd let her tell him what to do.

A moment later he heard her grunting. "Don't push too hard and break it," he told her.

"You think I don't know what I'm doing? It's my body."

"I'm just saying—"

"Well *just say* it to yourself," she mumbled. "If I get a goddamn yeast infection from these things, I swear I'm gonna kill you."

Johnny heard the first baggie squish into her wet hole. Curious, he peeked over his shoulder.

"Where'd you get that lube?"

"From my purse," she said.

"Why are you carrying around lube in your purse when I haven't touched you in over a month, Jenny?"

She gave him a really hard look, and said, "Is that any of your business anymore?"

She was right. He thought about it and he found he couldn't even muster up the energy to care. Whether she was just fucking Juicy to get smack or random strangers, it didn't matter anymore. They were through.

"Okay," she said, and he heard her grunt as she stood up to put her clothes back on. "It's done. Let's fucking do this."

Johnny turned to find her pulling up her panties. Her belt jingled as she stepped into her jeans. Her belly bulged a bit where the twenty-seven bags of heroin sat in her vagina but once she got her jeans zipped up he barely even noticed the difference.

"You got some makeup in there?" he asked her, pointing at her purse as she put the lube back.

"I need some?"

"You haven't had a shower in three days and you've been shooting up for a month. What do you think?"

Grumbling, Jenny made her way past him to the bathroom. From her expression in the mirror, he'd given her a sobering reality check. "You're right, I look like shit."

She started putting on blush, and somewhere during this Johnny pulled his attention away from the rich housewives fighting on the TV and caught her eye.

"I'm sorry, Johnny," she said, one eye closed to apply eye shadow. "This all got way out of hand. I just wanted us to have some fun, is all."

"We had some fun," he admitted.

"We did, didn't we?" She closed the other eye and applied makeup. "It wasn't all bad."

He agreed with a solemn nod, approaching the bathroom door.

Jenny smiled, but her smile turned into a wince. "Ow," she said. She said it again, only this time she dropped the makeup applicator in the sink and grabbed her abdomen.

"What? What is it?"

"*Cramps*," she moaned. "Oh God, it's real bad, Johnny."

She doubled over and stumbled out of the bathroom, then sat down on the bed and started breathing like they teach you in Lamaze class, like she's about to give birth. After what he'd just been through on the toilet, he could sympathize. He sat down beside her, worried for a second that she'd try to push him away again, but then she let out a pained, pitiful moan, like an animal dying in the woods, and Johnny knew she was beyond fighting.

"I'm gonna call an ambulance," he said, getting up for the rotary dial phone, but Jenny reached out blindly, begging him not to.

"I'll be... *fine*," she said, and then she groaned, "Oh God!" like she used to when she rode him cowgirl, the only way he could get her off, and her eyes rolled back, only the rest of her went back with them, falling onto the bedspread.

Johnny sat beside her, slapping her cheek to wake her up. Her eyelids fluttered but she didn't move, didn't make a sound. He pulled open one of her eyes. The pupil was huge, nearly as wide as the iris.

Panicked, Johnny put his mouth over hers and blew into it. Her lips were dry, and he couldn't feel her breath when he cupped his palm over them. He didn't know what to do. All those times he'd found her on the bed curled up like a baby it never once occurred to him to look up medical procedures for an overdose. He'd never even taken a single CPR class. Now she was dying, and even though he'd willed her to die a dozen times or more in the past month he couldn't just let it happen.

Johnny unzipped her jeans and tugged them down over her knees. He pulled down her panties, still damp and smelling like the chemical strawberry flavor of the lube and the tang of her unwashed pussy. Her dull eyes stared at the ceiling as he pushed through a tangle of pubic hair and stuck a finger inside of her, then two.

Without the lube, retrieving the bags would have likely been impossible. He thought if he could manage to get the bags out before more of them broke from her cramping and the heroin all seeped into her bloodstream, he might be able to save her life.

"Come on, Jenny, don't die, not now," he prayed.

Curling his hand into a beak shape, he pushed it in, his knuckles grazing against her pubic bone from the inside, the tight lip of flesh slipping over his thumb as he slid in up to the wrist. Once inside, he stretched his fingers to the outer edges of her hot fleshy canal, the dark pucker below widening and clenching under the pressure of his wrist. His fingers found one, feeling around blindly in the wet spongy tissue, then a second, and he pulled them out gingerly with a sucking sound, her hole remaining open like a look of surprise before closing to its normal size.

He put the baggies on the mattress and went back in for the others.

By the time he'd removed the second to last bag, her insides had started to cool, and the lube and natural lubricant her body had produced had thickened to a sticky white froth so it felt like stuffing a turkey. He couldn't find the broken bag, the one that had killed her. She might have pushed it up so far it broke from the pressure against her cervix. Or one of her fingernails had done it. He supposed he'd never know.

His fingers found something small and fleshy. He slipped it into his palm, holding it there with his thumb, and worked his hand back out.

Johnny's stomach rebelled when he opened his fist. He fell back on his ass, and the squishy, purplish thing plopped down wetly on the carpet.

Johnny shook his head.

It looked like a giblet, like something you might find in an egg yolk, only about an inch long. He couldn't tell if it was alive or dead. *Who's was it?* he wondered. Too mature to be Juicy's. It must have been at least eight weeks old from the length of it, and Johnny was pretty certain Jenny hadn't met the dealer until *after* she'd met Johnny.

Who's baby was it?

He didn't know. All he knew for sure was it

wasn't his.

He thought about fate, and choices, and of all the places in all the world, Juicy had to go and pick *this goddamn room* to meet.

According to the clock on the bed, Johnny had an hour and a half until the flight. He'd have to get there soon if he wanted to make it. And after all he'd been through, he realized he *wanted* to finish the job. He needed something to hold on to, something to take his mind off what had happened today, and everything that had lead up to it.

He'd never felt more empty than he did right now.

Best to finish packing.

Johnny swallowed the first white-crusted bag dry while the corpse of the woman he'd once loved stiffened beside him on the mattress, and her unborn child shriveled on the carpet.

Wash, rinse, repeat.

PRO(LAPSE)

SHYLA HAD SHIFTED uncomfortably further up on the bed so she was leaning up against the headboard, and was looking past him toward the bathroom. "Yuck," she said. "Well, I'd hate to talk about being dry after that story, but I could really use a glass of water."

Angel got up from his chair, went to the bathroom, removed the plastic cup from its paper covering, and filled it in the sink. He handed the cup to Shyla. She drank it greedily, and wiped her lips on her freckled forearm.

"Better?"

Nodding, she placed the emptied cup on the bedside table. "Better," she swallowed again. "What happened to Johnny? Did Juicy kill him, or did he deliver the package?"

"He delivered it. Juicy cleared the debt when Johnny got back to the States, and gave him an extra 'ten large' for what had happened to Jenny. I guess he felt guilty."

"That's good. Nobody deserves to die like that. I mean, she was a bitch, but I kind of sympathize. When a relationship is one-sided like that…"

"Oh?"

"Yeah," Shyla said. "I mean, maybe it wasn't like this with them, but when the love is unbalanced, when someone loves the other one more... that puts a lot of pressure on the one holding the power."

The thought hadn't occurred to Angel. He'd always suspected Jenny had started shooting up because Johnny hadn't been able to satisfy her needs. He liked Shyla's theory better, not that it would alleviate much of Johnny's guilt, nor lessen his pain. "So, you're saying Johnny put strain on their relationship because he asked too much of her?" he said. "That she started doing drugs because she couldn't give Johnny back the love he thought he needed?"

"It could be that," Shyla said. "I mean, it could be *anything*. Men and women, they act very different in their relationships, especially when it comes to sex. Men tend to blame the woman for all of their sexual problems, but a lot of the time, women blame themselves. I'm not saying that's how it was with Jenny and Johnny. Obviously she was a bit of a selfish bitch to put him through all that. But I like to look at things from all sides."

Angel nodded. "I wonder... do you think she knew she was pregnant?" He gave her a penetrating look. "Did she... have a *sense* of the baby inside her, or was it like luggage? Like the lube in her purse?"

Shyla appeared to give this some thought. "Well, I've never been pregnant, but I think mothers know."

She fumbled in her purse for another cigarette. "I think they do."

Angel nodded, hunkering down to unzip the backpack.

"Was Johnny a friend of yours or something?" she asked, lighting the smoke between her cherry red lips.

"Or something," Angel said, removing a large bottle of Slippin' Slide lubricant, the kind with a push top, and placed it behind him on the dresser.

The mattress squeaked as Shyla shifted again. "You don't have drugs in there, do you?" she asked with a grin.

"No drugs." He removed a small purple dildo from the bag and placed it beside the lube.

"You're gonna need a lot bigger than that to get *me* off, sweetie," Shyla scoffed.

"Do you have any piercings, Shyla?"

She ran the tongue stud over her teeth. "Just this. Have you ever had a blowjob from a girl with a tongue ring?"

Angel ignored the question, removing a floppy pink rubber fist from the bag by the forearm. He placed it on the table beside the dildo.

"That's a bit more like it," Shyla remarked with a grin. "How come you asked about piercings? Is that your thing?"

"Not exactly." He brought out a large black rubber cone and put it with the others.

"Now we're getting *serious*."

Angel stood up, looking over the sex toys on the dresser. "Do you know how they stretch a piercing?"

"Never really looked into it, no."

"They use a thing called a taper. The gauges, or sizes, go down in number the bigger they get. 20 gauge, 10 gauge, 5 gauge, etcetera. You have to let the wound semi-heal, then move up to the larger size, let it semi-heal again, move up to the larger size."

"Wash rinse repeat?" Shyla grinned.

"Wash rinse repeat." He nodded.

"So, are you saying you're going to try and stretch me?"

"If you're okay with that."

"I mean..." She seemed to consider it. "I do like to feel *full*."

"I'm glad to hear that," he said.

Her gaze fell to the crotch of his pants. "It doesn't look that big to me," she smiled, "but maybe you're a grower, not a shower."

Angel grinned. "I suppose we can skip the purple one." He pumped two squirts of lube into the palm of his hand, and lathered the rubber fist. "Take off your underwear, please," he said as he approached the bed with the now glistening sex toy.

Shyla did as directed, making a show of it as she raised her ass and reached under the mini dress to peel off her black G-string. She slipped the silky thing over her heavy hips and down her thick dimpled thighs, raising her legs and twiddling her toes as she wrestled them free. Instead of tossing them aside or laying them on the bedside table, she crumpled them into a ball and brought them to her face, smothering her nose and mouth with the lacy fabric and breathing in deeply, closing her eyes in delight, and Angel wondered if her panties were wet as the phantom itch in his groin resurfaced.

"Is it weird I love the smell of my own pussy?" she said, holding the panties out toward Angel. "Want some?"

"I gave up sniffing panties after prom."

"Your loss."

As Shyla tossed the bunched panties aside, Angel got down on the bed on his knees. She spread for him.

"Smooth as a baby's butt, isn't it?"

Aside from some cellulite her inner thighs were incredibly smooth, her labia and clit enclosed between two thick folds of slightly pinker flesh, already dewy with moisture. Angel agreed with a nod.

Shyla grasped the end of the fist, wiped off some lube into her hand, and spread it around her hole. Then she drew Angel's hand closer, until the end of the rubber fist pressed between her folds, widening them. The forearm bent as he pushed the toy inside her. She moaned as her pussy accepted the rubber arm up to the wrist.

"That feels *fucking good*," she breathed.

"Johnny did get back at Juicy, just so you know," Angel said, working the toy in and out with little enthusiasm, like a drill press operator on the night shift. "In case you were curious."

"*Oh*—" she groaned, "—*yyyeah?*"

"Mm-hmm. A couple of months later, in this same hotel room—"

JUICY STEPPED INTO Room 6 of the Lonely Motel, and kicked off his shoes by the door before turning to Chuck P., Johnny's porn director friend, who was screwing a video camera onto a tripod.

"I'm ready for my close-up, Mr. DeMille," he said, and giggled like a schoolgirl.

The room was already filled with guys, shirts and socks still on while they tugged on their dicks. Johnny had made sure Juicy wouldn't know anybody here except by their reputation on camera.

"Shit, Chuck-a-luck, you didn't tell me this was gon' be a sausage party," he said loud enough for the guys to hear, sidling close to where Chuck had set up the camera.

"It's a porn shoot," Chuck P. reminded him. "What did you expect?"

"Shit, man, I thought it was gon' be just me and the girl. You too, at *most*."

"What part of 'gangbang' did you not get?" Chuck P. asked, and Juicy put on his patented ice-cold look, but he knew Chuck P. had the upper hand since he could kick him out at any point, if he chose to.

"Okay," Juicy said, rubbing his palms together enthusiastically, "a'ight. Long as none of these dudes is a faggot, we cool."

"These are all professional actors," Chuck P. assured him. "If any one of them happened to be gay, he wouldn't touch *you* in a straight gangbang."

"Best *not*," Juicy said, and slapped an elbow into his fist.

"Look, if you don't want to be here…"

Juicy caught sight of the girl on the bed then, in between the guys pulling their puds. She was slim and black with big tits and a large booty, the way Johnny knew Juicy liked them. "I'll behave," he said, his eyes just about popping out of his head. "I'm a pro."

"No, you're not," Chuck P. told him. "You may know how to fuck, but in this business, you're an amateur. You've got a good stage name, though. That's a start."

Juicy sucked his teeth. "You know why they call me that, right? Because I make them bitches *squirt*, you know'm sayin'?"

The girl on the bed snorted laughter. Chuck P. just grinned and said, "We'll see about that."

See, Johnny knew Chuck P. from high school, and Chuck knew the girl on the bed well. He'd met her in a strip bar near the airport called The Canadian Ballet, an exclusive place catering to businessmen on layovers. A sex club, really, all word-of-mouth clientele, where this girl who called herself Candy Rains was like a human piñata some nights, and a lawn sprinkler on others. They used to hand out ponchos on those nights, but Juicy wouldn't be wearing a poncho, and the other guys were used to making fake female ejaculation videos, where the girl drinks a whole lot of wine coolers and masturbates, squeezing out pee in small bursts with her well-developed PC muscle as she cries out in ecstasy.

Johnny had something planned for Juicy that would make Poncho Night at The Canadian look like a honeymoon in Niagara Falls. Candy was game, as she'd participated in several of Chuck's previous films, and Johnny had paid for the shoot and the actors out of the money Juicy had given him when Jenny died. See, he didn't think what had happened was water under the bridge like Juicy seemed to. He made sure Chuck P. told the other guys what was up, but Juicy had no idea he was about to be voted King of Carrie's anal prom night—Chuck thought that was a pretty good title, if Juicy forced him to release it.

He set the camera rolling, and slapped Juicy on the back. "You better get in there before these other guys tear her ass apart," the director told him, aware of Juicy's anal fetish. It was what got Juicy asking Johnny about being in one of Chuck's movies in the first place, when he found *Ass Force 5* on Skinemax and recognized Chuck P.'s name.

Juicy rubbed his hands together with a papery sound that had gotten on Chuck P.'s nerves since they first met, and he stepped out of his track pants as he headed for the girl on the bed. She was playing with herself, using the same *come here* gesture she directed at Juicy on her g-spot with her other hand.

Juicy flipped her over on her stomach just like Johnny told Chuck P. he would, and hoisted her ass up in the air so she was resting on her knees with her tits pressed against the mattress. He spat into his hand, worked some onto his dick, then pushed a finger into her asshole.

Candy winced a little, not expecting him to dive right in, but she kept quiet. Chuck assumed she worried she might laugh if she said anything. Now that they were so close to launch, he had to bite his lip not to laugh himself.

He'd made sure to mix the red dye into corn starch and water nice and thick so it looked dark and ran sticky off the wooden spoon like blood. Some of it had spilled out of her asshole and dribbled down the inside of her thigh as he'd squirted it into her colon, but she'd wiped herself down well afterward, and had left no traces.

Her trick, which she performed twice weekly at The Canadian, was to give herself an enema before loading herself up with water and glitter, or milk, or whatever she'd decided would make the biggest splash, so to speak. Usually she would hold the liquids in her ass and solid objects in her pussy—like candy, or fruit, or ping pong balls—which was what had first caught Johnny's eye for obvious reasons. If he'd been blessed with such a strong sphincter as hers, he might have saved three lives that day in Room 6 instead of just his own.

So, Juicy rubbed the head of his cock up against

Candy's asshole, using the paintbrush technique— wax on, wax off—and then he got so eager he pushed it right in there. Candy, being the pro she was, just moaned and kept holding it in. Juicy closed his eyes and started licking and biting his lips, his pale, skinny ass cheeks flexing as he thrust his dick in and out of her dark, wet pucker.

The other guys crowded around squeezing their tools, less into the sex than awaiting the inevitable explosion. Chuck P. had asked them to wear white T-shirts and socks so the fake blood would show up nice and red for Juicy to see.

The man himself had lost himself in the fucking, which was a real treat for Chuck P. (and later for Johnny, watching on Chuck's brand-new HD television). Juicy gave her ass a good smack, watching it ripple, saying things like, "Yeah, girl," and "Take it, take that dick, take *all* of that white dick," as if it was the biggest, whitest thing she'd ever experienced, even though compared most of the other guys in the room, all professional porn actors and most of them white guys themselves, it was relatively average. Still, as far as acting went, he was a natural.

Candy opened the one eye that wasn't squished against the bedspread and looked at Chuck P., who cued her with a finger: Ground Control to Major Torrent. She clenched her jaw as she bore down, letting loose a huge blast around Juicy's wet dick like he'd pressed his thumb on the end of a hose, making the fake blood spray out in a thick, wide jet, covering Juicy from head to toe, dousing the guys standing around jerking their limp noodles, even splashing on Chuck's shoes from ten feet away.

There was a reason her stage name was Candy Rains—and now Juicy, dripping with glistening, sticky red liquid he definitely thought was blood, had a reason for his.

His eyes bugged out of his sticky red face and he started screaming, and some of the guys started backing away, looking like they were about to puke. Chuck saw what they were seeing, and nearly gagged himself: Candy's cherry red insides had oozed out of her, and as Juicy pulled out his dick they unrolled like an inside-out sock.

She'd prolapsed.

Juicy kept screaming. He stumbled off the bed, tripping over his own feet and grabbing up his drenched track pants on the way to the door, screaming, "*Oh shit, oh shit*," in a high-pitched squeal while he dripped and left bloody footprints all over the carpet. One of the actors actually puked, a guy who hadn't done many fetish videos before. That was a freebie for Johnny and Chuck P., and Juicy held back his own vomit with a hand as he scrabbled at the door handle, and ran out naked into the parking lot.

"YOU KNOW, ALL of these stories are really getting me hot," Shyla wisecracked.

"I can tell," Angel said, her vagina making sticky sounds as he pistoned the fist-shaped dildo in and out of her. "Think you're ready to move up a size?"

She shrugged. "I think maybe I could handle it."

She groaned as the fist came out of her with a wet pop. He brought it with him to the bathroom, where he rinsed it in the sink, and returned it to the backpack. He came back with the large black cone, the narrow end moistened with lube.

"Johnny blackmailed Juicy for fifty large not to release that video. Since he thought it would damage his reputation, especially the part where he screamed 'like a little bitch,' as Chuck put it, Juicy paid out, and Johnny never saw him again."

"So what happened to Candy?" Shyla wondered. "I gotta say, I feel a kind of kinship with her. With those pussy superpowers of hers, she sounds like a true icon."

"She was, in her own way. At the time, Candy didn't even realize her colon was hanging out of her like a giant pink larva until Chuck P. pointed it out to her," Angel said. "And when he did, all she said is, 'Oh, not again,' like it happened all the time, and sucked it right back into herself."

Shyla grimaced. "Honestly? That's one thing I don't get about porno these days. How do they have a whole genre based on a woman's asshole popping out? We sure have come a long way, baby."

Focused on the task at hand, Angel didn't respond as he knelt on the mattress.

"Jesus, that thing must be as big as your head," Shyla said.

Angel regarded the dildo, like a small parking cone dipped in black latex, with fourteen raised rings, each an inch wide, in addition to the rounded tip, an inch in width and length. "Not quite," he said. "Is it too big?"

"I think we could try it."

Angel pressed it against her sticky cunt. Her labia parted around it, accepting two inches, then three as the rubber widened.

"How do you know all these stories?" Shyla groaned, wincing as he pushed the dildo in deeper. "Do you work here or something?"

"We're old friends," Angel said.

"You and Johnny?"

"The motel and I," Angel said, deadpan.

"You're friends with a motel."

"You've never been friends with an inanimate object? A stuffed animal? A binkie?"

"I mean, I call my vibrator my 'special friend,' but we don't go see movies together, or gossip about hot boys."

Angel shrugged. "This Motel and I, we've both suffered great loss. This room in particular."

"Like the Whale lost Jonah?"

"Exactly like that."

"You know, I knew you were weird when I first met you, but this is like… if Weird was a serial killer, this right here would be his creepy basement."

Angel grinned and eased the dildo in another notch, making Shyla grunt. It was advertised to widen by a half an inch in diameter per ring, so that at its base it was an impressive eight inches wide. He found no pleasure in the experience; this was not for her pleasure or his own. If she enjoyed it, he supposed it was to his benefit. The more natural lubrication her body produced—the more of this toy she was able to accept—the better.

"I guess as far as sexual preferences go," Shyla said, "you telling a bunch of stories while you fuck me with dildos isn't that bad. Some guys like to choke. I *hate* that. And this one guy had me piss into a wine glass so he could drink it. Then he wanted me to toast him with my own glass of piss, and he wouldn't take no for an answer. I had to call my manager, Lars, to come and fuck the guy up."

"I'm sure you've got a lot of stories you could tell," Angel said.

"Oh, I could tell you some crazy ones. I've actually been thinking about writing them all down some day." She smiled. "*The Curvy Hooker.* You know, a play on the Xavier Hollander book? Or *Memoirs of a Full-Figured Geisha.*"

"I'm all ears," Angel said.

"They're pretty small, actually." When Angel gave her a quizzical look, Shyla said, "Your ears."

"Ah." Angel grinned. "If you're not in the mood to tell a story of your own, do you mind if I tell you another, while we play?"

Shyla shrugged. "Sure, why not? No more poop and prolapses, though, okay? I had a beef on weck for lunch, and it isn't sittin' all that well after Johnny's trip to the toilet."

"Fair enough," Angel said, and began his story.

<u>WOOM</u>

THE WOMAN OPENED the door to Room 6 of the Lonely Motel with its brand-new key fob on an incredibly warm day in December of 1980. Cautiously, she stepped over the threshold, holding her pregnant belly as she breathed in the smell of cigarettes and stale perfume.

Ray and Lola Baumgarten had bought this plot of land along Genesee Street in the hope of attracting flight attendants and businessmen on layovers after the 1977 expansion of Buffalo Niagara International's East Terminal, but business had never picked up the way they'd hoped. Eventually what was known then as The Paradise Motel came to be synonymous with drug deals and cheap trysts with prostitutes.

In March of 1979, under the weight of massive debt, Ray Baumgarten passed away from a coronary. His wife, who fell into a deep depression, changed its name to the Lonely Motel before hanging herself in Room 6 in the fall of 1980. Under new management, The Lonely Motel welcomed prostitutes and drug dealers with open arms by renting out rooms by the hour.

Mary Booker had rented Room 6 for two hours,

but she didn't expect to be there much longer than one. Her husband, Clevon, had left her shortly after she'd decided to keep the baby despite his objections. See, Mary had been raped on her way home from work—

"WAIT WAIT WAIT," Shyla said, holding up her hands. "You didn't say this was going be a rape story."

"It's not a rape story," Angel said. "Mary was raped, but that's just the, uh, what do you call it? The backstory. There's no rape in this."

Shyla narrowed her eyes. "Are you sure?"

"Is that a trigger for you, Shyla?"

"*Don't.*"

"Don't, what?"

"Don't get all smug about trigger warnings. I know they're bullshit, but can't a woman just not want to hear about rape without it being a goddamn *thing*? Every time you turn on the TV there's another woman getting raped and murdered. Every time you flick past the news it's 'rape culture on campus' and celebrity sex assaults and some new moral fucking panic. *Enough* already."

Angel hadn't expected such a tirade, but he supposed just because he was paying her to listen he shouldn't force that part of the story on her. She had a right to say 'no,' for now. "I was just setting the scene," he explained. "We can avoid it, if that's what you want."

Shyla nodded. "Please. Just... just fast-forward a bit, I guess."

FAST-FORWARD, THEN. Clevon didn't want her to keep the baby, but Mary was a good Christian girl who believed in the "sanctity of life." When Clevon left her, she still thought she could do it on her own. Mary was a big fan of *What's Happening!!*, and though it didn't look easy, she thought if Mabel could handle two kids on her own, she could handle one kid and part-time evenings at the Land's End Diner.

As time went by, her resolve weakened. She started to worry more. Violent crime rates kept escalating, and Mary began to wonder what sort of world she'd be bringing her child into; she only had to think about how it had been conceived to be reminded of it. By the thirtieth week of her pregnancy, her worry had grown into an obsession. She went to the hospital.

In 1970, New York State was the first to legalize abortions up to the twenty-fourth week. Despite the circumstances of her conception, Mary was too far along to legally have an abortion performed. They suggested she carry the fetus to term, and put him or her up for adoption.

Mary agreed that was what she would do, but she had no intention of carrying her child another day let alone twelve to fifteen more weeks. As she drove back to her flat from the hospital, she passed the blinking neon sign of the Lonely Motel. If ever there was a place she belonged right then, she thought, it was there.

The words HOURLY RATES caught her eye. She was naïve, despite her encounter, so she had no idea why a motel would have an hourly rate, nor why the man behind the desk, who wore a paisley shirt with a wide collar, and too much strong-smelling tonic in his hair and on his mustache, gave her and her swollen belly a lascivious look.

"Do the closets have clothes hangers?" she asked him.

He replied that customers expected hangers whether they spent the night or not, so they were provided free of charge.

"Yes, but are they *wire* hangers?"

He said he thought they were, and when the police asked him later why he didn't think to wonder why a woman in her condition might be inquiring about coat hangers, he reminded them that he was a desk clerk and not the Amazing Kreskin. He took her ten bucks and gave her the key, as he was paid to do by The Management. "Black, white, Chinese—all I care about is the green, you know what I mean?" he told them.

So, Mary entered Room 6 with a key whose fob brandished the motel's brand new name, and the man behind the desk thought about all the money he would make that evening from women turning tricks for businessmen on layovers who stopped by for a quick hump on their way to the Hyatt.

She sat down on the bed to remove her shoes. The mattress had a good bounce to it, she thought, not like the small, hard double she'd shared with Clevon, and had spent the last few months curled up on all alone, just trying to keep warm. She thought the room felt welcoming, as if it were whispering to her, lulling her into a false sense of peacefulness. Mary wrote all this and more down on the motel stationary, a letter she'd addressed *To my Unborn Child*.

It was the motel's idea for her to write the letter, according to her scrawled words—an indication of how deteriorated her mental state had become by then. She wrote about the assault, how she had tried to love and care for the child inside her despite how it had come to be, how she and her husband had argued day after day until he'd left her, how she'd tried to carry on with just the two of them when she couldn't be bothered to feed herself and get out of bed some days, and how she'd come to realize that her child was never meant to live. She feared for the future of the world, and "our children's children."

She wrote all this down, and signed it *Love, Mom*.

Then she rolled down her pantyhose.

She removed her pleated green wool skirt, and her slip. She slid down her nylon briefs. She unbuttoned her blouse, scowling at the vertical dark brown line that had appeared recently on her round belly, like a scar from her solar plexus through her navel to her pelvis. She folded the blouse and placed it on the bed alongside her stockings, slip and underwear.

Mary removed her Cross Your Heart bra (which the police bagged, only to file away among shelves of dust-covered evidence boxes, and later discard, the only indication it ever having been there an entry in an old ledger—*one Cross Your Heart bra, one pair women's nylon underwear, one pair tan hosiery*), and placed it with the rest of her clothing. She stood in front of the full length mirror, studying her newly curvy body, wondering how long it would take to get her figure back, wondering when the *linea nigra*—as the hospital OB/GYN had called it earlier in the day— would fade, if and when her breasts would return to their normal size.

She crossed to the bathroom and flicked on the light. Under the harsh bulb her eyes looked tired, her skin sallow, her hair coming loose from its tight bun. She turned on the water in the tub, and returned to the room.

On the bedside table she flicked on the clock radio, tuned to a modern rock station. When she did listen to music it was the oldies and classical, but she thought the rock music, if loud enough, would drown out any cries of pain she might make. The clock's red digital numbers told her she'd been in the room already for just over an hour.

The closet door opened silently on new hinges. The rack contained three hangers, two wire, and one wood with the paper dry cleaners' cover still on it. She grabbed one of the wire hangers, bending it as she returned to the bathroom. The sound of water splashing in the tub drowned out the radio, playing some song with a hillbilly twang about a girl named Bobby Sue and a boy named Billy Joe.

She stepped into the bath, careful not to slip. The water warmed her toes. The rest of her felt frozen, as if in response to the horror of what she was about to do.

Sitting down in the running water, she opened her legs with her knees raised. She'd managed to separate the two ends of the wire, where it coiled around the hook, and attempted to straighten out the bends.

She bent the hook into a sharper curve, her fingers turning pale from the pressure against the metal. As she brought the hooked end to her vagina, she felt the baby kick. Mary hadn't felt him kick since that morning, before her visit to the hospital, where usually he'd been quite energetic, and it made her wonder if he somehow *sensed* what was coming for him, the way Room 6 had sensed her presence, and welcomed her inside. It made her wonder if she was doing the right thing, or if she should get up right now, get dressed, and leave.

With the thumb and forefinger of her left hand, she parted her labia.

Her right hand began to shake at the thought of inserting the hanger. She'd bent the wire so the sharp end would snag the fetus or at least the umbilical cord for her to yank it out. It looked vicious, like the knife the man had used when he'd done those horrible things to her.

The metal parted her pink flesh, cold inside of her. She felt it pushing against her vaginal walls as she inserted it as far as her thumb, then fed in another inch, two, three, making her think of lowering a rope for a child stuck in a well, like that episode of *Emergency!* Mary had seen when she was still a girl.

I'm not hurting him, I'll be saving him, she thought, echoing the words she'd written in her letter. *Sparing him from a life of pain.*

The coiled end of the wire kept hitting the floor of the tub, her wrist sore from bending too far back. The angle was bad. She pushed herself to her feet, holding the wire carefully so as not to drastically change its angle, and prevent it from coming out.

The baby kicked her several times in a row as she stood, as if fending off an attack with karate. Grinding her teeth against the pain, she pressed her free hand flat against the wall tile and raised her left leg onto the rim, still holding the wire with her right hand.

Vaguely, above the splashing water, she heard John Lennon moaning for two or more of his fans to come together over him, and assumed it was a sex reference. Everything was about sex these days. Mary thought it was no wonder the psychopath had felt compelled to do what he had to her.

She fed in the wire. In a moment, it struck something firm and spongy. With no concept of her inner workings, she supposed she must have pushed it in too far. The baby must have been close. Mary gave it one last hard push, felt the flesh inside her part and the wire move freely before stopping again.

The baby kicked wildly, shifting around much more than he ever had before.

Relieved, Mary twisted the wire, moving it back and forth, hoping to snag him and drag him out of her. Pain erupted in her abdomen, and Mary lost hold of the wire. It remained hanging out of her, wobbling like a doorstop as she tried to steady her breathing.

The first drops of blood dripped from the end of the wire and splashed pink into the water below. Overcome by a sudden grand terror, Mary slowly lowered her quivering leg as more blood began to pour out of her, thin and running down her inner thighs, mixing with the water at her feet. Using both hands to grasp the wire, she tried to pull it out as gingerly as possible despite the violent tremors in her fingers.

It wouldn't budge.

She tugged, and another sharp pain flared, far worse than the first. The bottom of the tub looked like feeding time at the shark tank. Mary felt woozy, like she might pass out at any moment. The way she saw it, she had two choices: pull the wire out and potentially bleed to death in this tub, or leave the wire inside her, dress around it (she felt certain it would end up poking out of the bottom of her skirt, like a thin metal tail), and somehow get herself to the hospital.

She imagined the doctor's impatient glare. She thought about what his older white nurse would think of her, a black woman with a coat hook in her vagina, giving herself a back-alley abortion like some common street trash. Who knows? They might even assume it was a sex thing. Everything was about sex these days. No one knew it more acutely than Mary.

No—she would have to get the wire out herself.

The baby struggled as she pushed the wire deeper inside of herself, as delicately as she could muster with her fingers shaking so badly. She couldn't tell which side of the wire was barbed. She hoped, as she pressed the metal against what she assumed was her cervix, that she'd done so with the smooth side.

And she *pulled*…

The wire came out of her with a springy twang, bringing more blood with it. But it was *out*. She was *free*.

Breathing a prayer to Jesus, she bent to put the warped hanger on the toilet seat.

As she bent she slipped on the slick ceramic floor and fell forward. Her head struck the tile and she slid down the wall, her forehead striking the hot water knob, splitting open, her front teeth smashing against the faucet. She fell into the tub, but even though the water was shallow, there was no saving Mary. She was already unconscious by the time she landed face-first in the running water.

ANGEL FELT SHYLA'S body shudder through the hand he used to work the dildo. "That story made my pussy want to shrivel up like a salted snail," she said.

"Do you want to take a bweak for a while?" Angel asked, and bit his lip, hoping she hadn't caught his unintended lapse.

"How about *forever*?"

"Hmm. How about a ciga— a ciga*rette*?" he said, deliberately forming the word to preserve the *R*.

"That might help. Grab my purse?"

Angel got up and handed her the purse from the bedside table. As she reached into it, the dildo slipped out of her a notch, still inside her up to the top of the eleventh ring: ten inches deep, five inches wide. He'd lucked out when the agency sent Shyla. Her cunt was an absolute marvel.

The other women, even those who'd had several children through natural birth, had only been able to stretch the girth of a baseball bat or a liquor bottle. Shyla, by some miracle, could stretch so wide he thought she might be able to accept what he had to give her.

Her gifted pussy would allow her to receive his gift to her.

She lit two cigarettes, handing one to Angel, dragging on the other. He thanked her, still staring at her beautiful vagina. She exhaled a wispy gray cloud. As her belly shifted, the dildo stayed put.

"Was the baby okay?"

"He survived. Once her two hours were up, the desk clerk came into the woom—*room*," Angel corrected himself, "and found her in the tub. She was braindead by the time the paramedics arrived. She died in the hospital a few days later.""

With a scowl, Shyla said, "I don't mean to be rude, but... did I just hear a lisp?"

"It's not—" Angel shook his head. "—it's not a lisp. A lisp is when you pronounce *S* like *T-H*."

"Right, sorry. What is it called then?"

"Speech therapists call it rhoticism," he told her, "or derhotacization. It took me a long time to master saying my *R*s for some reason when I was a kid. But it's not a lisp."

"Okay. I mean, you seem fine with it now."

"It's usually fine, just... sometimes it comes out when I'm stressed."

"Well, it could be worse."

"Could it?"

Shyla shrugged. "It's just something you say. *Could be worse*. I mean, it could *always* be worse, right? You could have been born brain damaged. You could have... I don't know, been born with two heads, or a little arm."

"*Phocomelia*," Angel said. "I don't think it would be that bad. Aside from only being able to jerk off with one hand."

Shyla snickered. The room sat silent until she noticed the traffic out in the street, and turned toward the blinds. "You know, I always wanted to be a mother," she said.

"Oh?"

"Mm-hmm. Never happen though." She shrugged. "I'm kind of okay with that."

"Why not?"

"When I was younger, I... well, a lot of damage was done to my lady parts, and I had to have an emergency trachelectomy."

"Trachel—?"

"—ectomy. Removal of the cervix."

"Ouch," Angel said.

"It wasn't that bad. Expensive, though. My dad went into debt to pay for it, that's how come I started doing this. I was bleeding internally. We had to get it done. Only problem is, it didn't heal right. So now I've got an extra deep vagina."

"That doesn't seem like much of a problem to me."

Shyla shrugged. "Well, it's hard to feel satisfied by an average-length penis when your pussy just goes on forever."

"Like the Delaware Aqueduct," Angel remarked. "I'm sorry to hear that, Shyla. Maybe we can rectify that today. Tit for tat."

"And tat for tits." Shyla grinned, cupping her heavy breasts and squeezing them. Her cherry red lips formed an O as Angel pushed the dildo deeper. "Bad angle," she grunted, and Angel pulled it out a notch.

"Sorry," Angel said, getting up from the bed to sit

in the chair opposite. "What's the weirdest thing a client has ever asked you to do?"

"I mean, this is up there, don't get me wrong." Shyla winked. "Kidding. Let's see, there was the diaper guy, and the pee drinker…" Her eyes alighted. "Oh! There was that guy who was into queening."

"Queening?"

"Facesitting," she explained.

"Oh," Angel said, and fell silent.

"I can't believe I forgot," Shyla said. "The sub lies on his back, and the dom sits on his face, covering his nose and mouth with her pussy and butthole so he can't breathe. The woman is in complete control, except like most BDSM stuff there's an out, a safe word, but with facesitting it's a little different. The guy can't actually talk because he's being smothered, unless he's a pussy whisperer or something. So he's got to tap out—you know, like in a wrestling match?"

Angel nodded, listening intently, smoking faster so the minty tobacco would smother the strong chemical smell that arose from his memories.

"So this guy, he was really into facesitting, so much that he had this thing he called a 'smother box'—" Off Angel's quizzical look she explained, "Basically it's this nice wooden box with a pillow on the inside, and a hole on the top like the ones on a massage table. This thing was really elaborate. I'm pretty sure he made it himself. It had all kinds of engravings on it, too. Like ancient Chinese and Indian pornographic etchings. I don't know if they were replicas or just something he had someone do for the box. Maybe he did them himself, I don't know."

"That's dedication."

"That's what *I* said. Anyway, aside from the smother box, he wasn't all that out of the ordinary. You know, no obvious red flags."

"Red flags?"

"Danger signs. 'Do not pass Go, do not collect two hundred dollars.' Although I charge two-hundred and sixty, and I usually expect a tip," she added with another wink.

"Danger signs—like what?"

"Well like, do they exhibit odd behavior. I mean, a lot of clients—we never call them *johns*, that's what cops call them—a lot of them are weird, or socially awkward, but I mean things like, do they try to coerce you into doing things you've explicitly said you won't do. Do they look like a cop, because cops still harass us even when we're not getting our business on the street. Do they," she thought a moment, "do they try to get you to secluded areas instead of their apartment or a hotel. Do they act drunk or high, or do they behave erratically—as opposed to *erotically*," she added, grinning slightly at her silly little joke. "The guys with the fetish gear and whatnot, we don't usually have to worry about. They're there for the act. Most guys are there for the woman, but the fetish guys… they know what they want and the woman is just an accessory."

Angel nodded thoughtfully. "You seem to know a lot about people. Are you in school?"

Shyla grinned. "Paying my way through college, right? Not this girl. You'd be surprised how much you can learn about people if you're paying attention."

"I don't doubt it. So how could you tell I wasn't a danger?"

"Well, first off, you called me to a motel, and even though the Lonely has a bit of a reputation, it's a known place. Dispatch probably already checked you off for red flags when she heard where you were staying. Plus, you were specific about what kind of woman you wanted."

"So are serial killers," Angel remarked.

"True, but you also said you'd hired from the agency before and didn't get what you wanted."

"The dispatcher told you that."

"Uh-huh."

"I could have been lying."

"There's that chance, sure. But why lie about that?"

"I suppose."

"When I *got* here, there was a big red flag. For me, anyway."

"Oh?"

"You shook my hand. Some guys kiss it, the way men used to, but the first and pretty much only time I've ever had my hand shook by a client he ended up trying to beat the shit out of me while we were fucking, so I've been wary of hand-shakers ever since."

"Interesting."

"Also, you're African-American. Light skinned, but it's pretty obvious you're not Latino or Tonawanda Indian, or anything like that."

"Okay," Angel said with a smirk. "So why was that a good thing?"

"Well, everybody knows serial killers are mostly white. You're also well-dressed, which isn't necessarily good or bad, but in your case I saw it as a good sign."

"Why?"

"Because of the scar."

Curious, Angel asked, "What about my scar made you trust me?"

"With the clothes, it gave you a look of vulnerability. I thought a psychopath would be too vain not to cover it up with manscara, especially someone as well-groomed as you are."

"That's an interesting evaluation. Anything else?"

"Well, your bag of tricks," Shyla said, nodding toward it, "it was a little off-putting at first. I mean, for all I knew, you had a dead body cut up in pieces inside there. Especially with that smell, when I first stepped in? Woof. But then you took out the lube, and the toys, and I knew you were safe."

"How so?"

"Aside from the size of this one, there was nothing out of the ordinary."

"No smother boxes, as far as you could see," Angel said with a toothy grin.

"And no *diapers*, which is a definite plus."

Smiling, Angel said, "So why don't you tell me about the Smother Man?"

"Okay," Shyla said, seemingly pleased to get to tell a story of her own. She stubbed out her cigarette, and began.

(S)MOTHER

THE SMOTHER MAN opened the door and right off the bat he wouldn't hold my gaze. He kept his eyes down most of the time I was in his hotel room, staring at my tits, or my stomach and ass, and I could tell this was going to be an interesting experience. As far as red flags went, I didn't see anything too off-putting. There was a strange box on the bed that didn't seem like it came with the room, but that was it. I thought it looked like some kind of religious relic, like maybe it had an ancient Bible inside it, or a lock of some old dead Pontiff's hair.

"What's in the box?" I asked him, and he looked over at the box like he'd forgotten about it.

He goes, "Nothing," in this quiet little voice like a kid who's been scolded. He wandered over to it and flipped it over, showing me the hole in the lid with a proud smile, flicking his eyes up to mine for a half a second before looking down at the floor.

For some reason the hole in the top reminded me of a confession box. Like if I peeked inside I'd see Father Dennison, my old priest, looking out at me. That thought really creeped me out, but I wasn't going to let it cost me an hour's work.

"Is that a jewelry box?" I asked.

The guy just shook his head, and I saw some dandruff fall from his greasy hair and land on his shoulders like snow.

"Well, what is it then?" I go, getting really annoyed at that point because it seemed like he was never going to tell me about the box. I felt like Brad Pitt in that movie about the serial killer, and thinking about serial killers and my old priest was definitely not putting me in the mood to fuck.

"I call it my *smother box*," he kind of whispers, and he raised his eyes just enough to dart around the hem of my skirt.

Looking at the box again, right away I could see how it worked. It was like those medieval punishment things, what do you call them? The stocks, yeah. I could see where the hinges were, and the neck hole in the side. Close the box around the sub's head, and the dom sits on the little hole like on an outhouse toilet.

"You want me to smother you?" I asked him.

His nod was so timid I was barely sure he'd made it.

"Well, okay," I said, "why don't you put it on for me?"

His eyes pretty much popped out of his head when I said that, and a tiny little smile creeped onto his pimpled face. He looked about thirty-five, maybe forty. He was wearing this ugly sweater, I guess would have called it a Cosby sweater before saying

Ralston

the name "Cosby" started to feel sleazy. A little thick around the middle, but honestly, I figured it was more likely a weakness for Little Debbie snack cakes than a beer gut from the way he carried himself, and he wore his pleated pants so high at the bottom I could see the tops of his white tube socks under them, above a dirty pair of sneakers.

He plucked the box up from the bed and took it with him to the bathroom. This was a pretty decent hotel he'd paid for, with a sitting room in front and, from what I could see through the bathroom door when he opened it, a pretty large tub. I thought he might let me stay and have a soak if I didn't have to jet off to another client. I wondered what kind of bath balls they'd have in a ritzy place like that. I mean, I make a decent living as an escort, but I don't usually treat myself to places like that. I'm saving up so I can go live some place where the beaches are hot and the guys are even hotter.

Nope, never travelled outside of the area. Went across the border a couple of times to Niagara Falls, but that's about it. I'm a Buffalo gal, born and bred.

When the Smother Man came back into the bedroom, his small pimpled face was sticking out from the front of the box. He looked like a cuckoo clock, and I laughed a little thinking that, even though they tell you on your first day never to laugh at clients. I just couldn't help it. The thought of him going "*Cuckoo! Cuckoo!*" while he stuck out his tongue to lick my pussy just got me laughing, and when I get laughing it's hard to get me to stop.

Well, the poor guy hung his head, and I realized I'd humiliated him, so I gave him an apology. He just goes, "Don't apologize. I know I look stupid," and honestly, I just wanted to hug the little bastard at that point, he was so sad and cute, even though I couldn't imagine actually hugging him without getting his dandruff all over my nice top, but at least his greasy head was locked inside the box.

What he said made me understand what he was looking for, though. He was a sub, and he wanted me to berate him. He wanted me to lay down the law, so I did.

"Get on the bed," I shouted at him, pointing at it.

He kind of shrank away from me, his head dropping down into his shoulders like a turtle, only it couldn't go far because of the box. He goes, "Yes, ma'am," and headed for the bed.

"Yes, *Mistress*," I scolded him, and he repeated it. "On your knees!"

He goes, "Yes, Mistress," again, and got down on his hands and knees like a dog to crawl the rest of the way to the bed.

I told him to climb up, and he did. I told him to roll over on his back, and he did that too. Then I moved over to the bed myself and stood with my knees against the mattress, right about where his head was. The thing about these guys who love queening, they need to see the pussy from below. It's like—you know how in movies when someone does the sign of the cross and prays in front of Jesus, and they always point the camera down at the guy praying, and point it up at Jesus? That's what this is like. He wanted to worship my pussy. The smother box was his confessional.

So real slowly, I slipped off the frilly black underwear I was wearing. I used to have a bush back then, since some guys were requesting it because it was making a comeback in porn but their wives were all still sporting hardwood floors because of what porn told them to do in the '90s. I'd spritzed a real fragrant perfume down there, and it mixed well with my natural smell. I kicked my panties aside and squatted down so my bush tickled his forehead.

"You want this?"

The box moved up and down on my inner thighs when he nodded.

"Beg for it," I told him.

He knew just what to say, as if he'd practiced it a hundred times. "*Please, Mistress. Please sit on my face. Smother me Mistress, pleeeeease.*"

So I got up onto the mattress, my legs on either side of him, and I squatted over the box. Sitting down on it was uncomfortable, but I didn't let it show. I was in charge, and if I whimpered or whined, I would look weak. He wanted me to be *strong*.

His face was mashed up against my pussy. When he breathed in through his nose it sounded like he was blowing a fart against his arm. It tickled, but I didn't laugh. I was a no-nonsense bitch. I was *The*

Good Wife. I was *Xena: Warrior Princess.*

We'd worked out that he would tap me on the thigh when he was ready for me to get off of him, when he'd had enough or he needed some air. His arms were flat at his sides when I felt his tongue flick out and lick my pussyhole.

"Put your dirty tongue back in your mouth!" I shouted at him, and immediately I felt it retreat, like a penis in cold water. "Nobody said you could lick my pussy, you worm. Get back in the dirt," I said, inspired when I'd improvised the word *worm*, and I slid my sticky pussy down to his chin, hunching over to rub my asshole on his nose. "Breathe it in, worm. Rub your nose in my dirty shithole."

He did just like I told him to, and when he breathed out again I felt it tickle my pucker. I almost giggled then but I was too far into character by then. Grade twelve drama class finally paying off.

I felt a tentative touch on my thigh, and raised my ass off his face to give him some air.

"Thank you, Mistress," he gasped.

"You'd best do better than that next time," I lectured him. "You'd better take a deep breath before you dare to lick my pussy again."

I felt the box move up and down on my inner thighs as he nodded.

"Are you ready?" I asked him.

Again, the box moved. I heard him suck in a deep breath.

I sat down on the box and squirmed on his face.

His tongue came out and this time I let it search my folds for my clit. He found it—I'm not sure if it was by accident or experience, and it stayed there, circling it, flicking it. I was tripping on power already, and honestly, this was the best my pussy'd ever been licked, even counting the handful of times I'd doubled up on clients with another girl and she ate me out. It was like he was reading hieroglyphs with his tongue, like he was speaking to my clit in some ancient language. Vaginese, or something.

This was my pussy whisperer.

When I came, I gushed buckets. Candy Rains would have been proud of me that day. I mean, I waterboarded that poor bastard like it was shower time at Guantanamo. Honestly, it was the first and last time I'd ever squirted from clitoral stimulation alone, and I was pretty spent. My pussy was numb, my thighs were quivering, and my fucking legs felt like they were made out of JELL-O.

I raised up onto my knees, only then just realizing I hadn't felt his tongue wriggling down there in maybe a minute. I thought maybe he was just letting me cum at my own pace, but then I started to get worried. I slid off the bed, my legs still shaking, and looked down at the man in the box.

He looked just like a little baby, his face all wet and purple inside the hole. I slapped his nose a few times and he didn't flinch, his eyes didn't open, so I got down and started doing CPR, which I learned because some of my clients are a bit older now that everyone's taking Viagra, and I thought it would save me a lot of trouble if one of those old fart's happened to have a heart attack while we were in the middle of fucking, like that '90s movie with Madonna and the Green Goblin.

Well, the poor guy's eyes shot open finally, and he coughed out a mess of salty-tasting liquid right into my mouth, which I guess was my cum, and while he choked, his face started going back to its normal color, and I unlatched the box and flipped open the lid, hoping it wasn't cutting off his circulation.

He gasped, and he laughed. At first I thought his eyes were just shiny from my cum or from lack of oxygen, but when he sat up tears started spilling down his face.

"That was the most... *intense* thing I've ever experienced," he said, louder than he'd said anything since I first stepped into the room, almost like he'd finally found his voice, and he took my hands in his and kissed them. He goes, "*Thank* you," and kissed them again, gushing about as much as I just did on his face. "*Thank* you, you have no idea how much you helped me!"

"HE WAS BORN again," Angel remarked.

"Yeah, I guess he was," Shyla said, and shook her head at the memory. "He told me he was on the verge of suicide. He was so obsessed with this idea of what he wanted, and nothing ever came close until he found me. When I sat on his face, he said it was like a religious awakening."

"And when you came, it was his baptism."

Shyla snickered. "I was so happy for him, I didn't want to ruin it telling him it was the first time I'd ever done it. I wanted to... maintain the illusion, you know what I mean?"

Angel smiled. "I think I do."

"Can you imagine that, though? Being so fixated on a fetish you'd kill yourself if you knew you'd never experience it?"

"I can," he said. "It's certainly not *rational*. Then again, few things about sex are."

"I don't know," Shyla said, cocking her head to the side. "When you think about all the war, greed, murder, drug addiction, crime... those 'bad things' you mentioned. Sometimes sex seems like the *only* sane thing people do. I mean, it's simple. It's usually a mutually beneficial transaction, as long as it's consensual. Even when you don't cum, it's still *sex*."

"You make a good point," Angel said. He pushed up from the chair. "And on that note, let's get back to work."

"Agreed. This pussy ain't gonna fuck itself."

Nestled between her legs, Angel said, "As luck would have it, I've also got a story about smothering."

"Of course you do," Shyla said, rolling her eyes.

"Do you not want to hear it? It didn't happen in this room, but I think it's germane."

"*Germane?*"

"Relevant," he said.

"Honestly? I'm kind of more interested in your stories now than what you might have waiting for me inside your pants."

Angel laughed, and then he said—

THERE WAS A boy who grew up without his parents, and when he was a man he drifted aimlessly through life. No real goals. Few attachments. He'd only loved two women aside from the mother he'd never met, and both of them had betrayed him just like his mother had by abandoning him.

The boy who grew up to be an angry man blamed all of his troubles on the mother he had never known. Therapy didn't help. Church groups bored him. Drugs and alcohol were merely bandages on open wounds. When he saw the ad in the newspaper, he thought he'd finally found a chance to turn things around.

OVERCOME YOUR ANGER! the headline said, and below that, in smaller type: *Rebirthing can CHANGE your LIFE! Join us to begin YOUR new life TODAY! Serious applicants ONLY! Send a check for $1 to…* Below the copy was a P.O. Box, the way all of those ads used to have P.O. Boxes, and no phone number. He thought this was a little suspicious, but all he had to lose was a buck and a stamp, so he wrote to them, expecting to lose the dollar and never hear back.

Two weeks later, he got a letter in the mail. No return address. His name and address printed in dot matrix on the front of the envelope. He tore it open, but it felt empty. He squeezed it so it opened wide, and shook it over the kitchen counter.

A little scrap of paper fell out. An address and a date, *Thursday 8P.M.*

He showed up at the address a few minutes early, and knocked on the door of the apparently abandoned factory, expecting no one to answer. He ignored the van that pulled up to the curb, until the passenger rolled down the window and said, "Have you come to be reborn?"

Suspicious, the man said he had.

"Well, hop in the back. This is Janis," the shaggy haired white guy in an army green duffel coat said, nodding toward the driver, an aging Asian lady with hippie braids and round John Lennon glasses. "I'm Irv. We're attachment therapists."

The man took a wary step back from the van.

"Look, do you want help, or not?" Irv said with a bored sigh.

"I've tried therapy," the man said.

"Not like this, you haven't. They call it the Evergreen Method. Were you by any chance adopted?"

The man shook his head. "I lived in a foster home until I was sixteen," he said.

"Both parents, huh?" Janis said, lighting a thin brown cigar. "That's a real drag."

"Look, this would be a lot easier if you got in the back," Irv said, squinting out at the yellow streetlight.

The man considered it. He'd come out all this way on the bus just to meet them. Felt silly to go all the way back home just because the meeting was in a van instead of an abandoned factory, as if one were any worse than the other.

He got in the back. It smelled of patchouli, some kind of cheap men's body spray, and sweat, as Irv leaned over the back of the seat.

"Hey, man, glad to have you aboard." Irv stuck out a hand, and the man shook it, while Janis eyed him in the rearview mirror. "Just pop a squat on the rug," Irv said, indicating the rolled up rug on the otherwise empty floor.

The man sat. Janis threw the van into drive, and eased away from the curb. They drove through the darkened streets in silence for a bit.

"So what does this…?"

"Evergreen?" Irv asked.

The man nodded. "What does it entail?"

"It's a proven method. Janis and I both went through it ourselves. Janis's mother died when she was twelve. She got into drugs and starting fires and whatnot, until Evergreen saved her life." In the mirror, Janis locked eyes with the man, and gave him a stern nod. "Me, I've been fighting all my life. Never was a good kid. Truth be told, I was a real asshole. My parents took me to see a therapist, Dr. Schwartzman. Totally turned my life around."

(79)

The man gave Irv the look of appreciation he supposed was required.

"That's why we do what we do," Irv said. "To give back. Pay it forward, so to speak."

Janis nodded as she sped up to beat a yellow light.

"Your parents," Irv said, "did you know them?"

"I never met my mother."

"And your daddy?"

"Never in the picture," he said.

Irv nodded as if he'd heard it all the time. "You always been angry?"

"As long as I can remember." The man shrugged. "It didn't really occur to me it was something I could change until I saw your ad."

"That's rad," Irv said, and the man had to chuckle.

Janis pulled the van into a Dunkin' Donuts lot, and the back doors opened. Another man and woman stepped in, and the man of the couple was so tall he had to crouch.

"Didn't expect you to be a brother," the older black man said. "How you doin'?"

"I'm fine," the man said.

"He fine," the tall man chortled. "You hear that, Janis?"

Janis ignored him, pulling the van out of the lot and merging into traffic.

"Don't pay any attention to Victor," the young woman said. "I'm Raylene." She extended a bejeweled hand, her blonde cornrow beads rattling as she leaned forward. The man shook it. "Real pleasure," she said.

Raylene sat beside the man. Victor sat crossed-legged across from them, leaning against the wall.

"Hey, Vic," Irv said, "my man here was just telling Janis and me about how he grew up in a foster home. Victor grew up in a white family, you believe that shit? Like a reverse Oreo."

Victor grinned. "Yeah, it was just me and Willis, and a sexy little redhead." He laughed. "Whatchoo talkin' 'bout, Irvine?"

Irv cracked up. "That gets me every time."

Raylene rolled her eyes. Janis drove with hers on the road.

"You guys seem like one big happy family," the man said, anxious to fill the silence.

Victor laughed. "It's a dirty job, but someone gotta do it."

Irv laughed with him, and held out a hand to slap him five.

The brakes squealed as Janis parked. The front windshield was dark. The man had no idea where they'd taken him until the windows began to rattle as something boomed by above them. The sound became a screeching, and then he knew: they'd parked near the airport. A jet had just passed overhead.

The vinyl seats grumbled as Irv slipped between them, and hunkered down in the back between Victor and Raylene. "Next stop, Wombtown," he said, and the others chuckled.

"What does that mean?" the man asked, growing nervous.

"It means, we gon' roll you up in this carpet and let you fight your way out," Victor explained. With the dome light out, his smile seemed incredibly white against his dark skin.

"Like a little baby," Raylene said, and then made this little *tee hee* sound when she laughed.

The man got up to leave, but Irv grabbed him by the shoulder and sat him down again. "You ain't goin' nowhere," he said. "We had an arrangement."

"You asked for it," Raylene said. "We're just giving you what you want."

"Well, maybe I changed my mind." The adrenaline poured like acid into his veins. Heart pounding. Were they a cult? Were they going to let him live? "Haven't you ever changed your mind about something you thought you wanted?" he asked them—*pleaded* with them.

"I told you he'd pussy out," Janis said.

"I'm not pussying out," the man said. He promised himself he wouldn't let them bully him into submission. He *wouldn't*.

"Unroll the carpet," Victor said.

"Rug," Irv corrected him.

"Are we gon' have this argument every damn time?"

"If you keep calling it rug, we are. Carpets go wall to wall," Irv said, gesturing the expanse with his hands. He pointed to the object in question. "*That* is an area rug."

"He's right," the man said.

"You supposed to be on my side," Vic said, glaring at their passenger. "High yellow-ass nigga."

"I'm not on a side. I don't even want to *be* here."

"You messaged us," Raylene cooed. "You *paid* us to be here. To *save* you."

"C'mon, just get in the rug, man."

"Yeah. Get in the carpet."

Irv narrowed his eyes at Victor as Raylene raised up on her feet and unrolled the rug. It smelled like a musty old closet as it flapped out dustily over the man's shoes. He stepped back as if the fabric was a blood puddle he was trying to avoid.

He turned to face Irv, who nodded toward the rug encouragingly. Then Victor, who only scowled. Raylene smiled at him.

The man got down on his hands and knees. He laid down flat on his front.

"Hands at your sides," Irv instructed, and the man did as he was told, cursing himself for going along, for getting in the van with these weirdos in the first place, for sending the damn dollar, for reading the fucking ad.

Victor and Irv began to roll him up in the rug. Darkness enveloped him. He sucked in as much air as he could—he'd learned to hold it for long periods of time on the swim team in high school—filling his lungs with the cloying smell of dust. They rolled him over once, twice, three times, until he was wound tightly within the fabric, and he thumped into the wall of the van.

Little by little light began to fade in from the far end of the rolled-up rug. He had a moment to think, *This isn't too bad…*

And then someone sat on his chest.

His breath *lunged* out of him. Someone else sat on his ass, squashing his crotch against the floor, and another on his legs. He was trapped. He was sweating, stifled by his own exhalations.

He suddenly realized the similarity between the words *womb* and *tomb* wasn't a coincidence.

"*I can't breathe…*" he gasped, as audibly as the small amount of air in his lungs would allow.

Struggling, he tried to raise himself off the floor. Feet kicking, his legs wouldn't budge. Arms plastered to his ribs. He tried to roll, rocking himself back and forth, but the weight of them was too much. He screamed, practically voiceless, like crying out in a nightmare.

The windows began to rattle as another jet passed.

Weeping now, taking in little sips of dusty air, heart hammering like a piston, he made one last futile struggle, and his whole body deflated. All of his remaining energy vanished. He stopped moving.

"C'mon, man, *fight!*" Victor's voice sounded like it was travelling to him from space, like a weak satellite signal from a far-off star system. Irv joined him, sitting atop his legs. "*Fight*," he said.

"You can do it, honey," Raylene said, muffled, sitting on his pelvis.

With the last of his strength, the man threw his elbows at the inside of the rug. He twisted. He kicked. Inching himself toward the opening. Dragging toward the light.

Irv's weight slipped off his legs. He pressed forward, using his feet to propel himself, the light at the end of the tunnel widening. Dilating.

"Push!" Irv shouted.

Blessed cool air tickled his scalp.

"*Push*," Victor urged.

The dark flap of rug revealed his eyes.

"PUSH!" Raylene cried.

He *pushed*.

As he crowned, and his lips were finally exposed to the heaven-sent patchouli stink of the van once more, he sucked in a huge breath.

Victor's weight withdrew from his chest. Raylene got to her feet. He struggled his way out, the rug unfolding as he pushed with his elbows and kicked, until he lay there, entirely free, sweating, taking in hungry gulps of air.

When his strength returned, he pushed himself to his hands and knees and scurried into a corner, worried they might try to capture him again, worried this time he wouldn't be able to free himself.

"*You did it*," Raylene said, smiling with tears in her eyes. Victor raised a fist and said, "*My* man!" Irv began a slow clap. In the rearview mirror, Janis met his eyes, and nodded.

"Fuck you people," he said, still breathing heavily, hugging his knees to his chest.

Raylene's smile drooped. Victor lowered his fist, his brow furrowing. Irv stopped clapping with his hands at their widest distance.

"We were only trying to help…" Raylene said, her voice small.

"*Help?* You nearly fucking killed me. If you think that's help, you people need serious counselling."

"Fuck you, man," Irv said. "We did this for *you*."

"No fuck *you*," he said, further enraged by the tears streaming down his face. "You did this for *yourselves*. You think you're so fucking *enlightened*? Fucking *righteous*? *Bullshit!* Go to Hell."

They looked back at him with their mouths agape. He felt along the door.

"I'm getting the fuck out of here," he said, pulling feebly on the handle. Wiping his tears with the back of his hand, he jerked the handle, and the door came open to the sound of traffic. He stumbled out into the gravel lot. Off to the left of the van, the airport lights shined brightly into his eyes through the tall wire fence, his tears creating stars. He blinked violently.

"You need to let go of that anger, man," Victor said.

"You need to shut the fuck up, you hypocrite! If any of you try to contact me again, if you come to my house, I will *fuck* you up. You hear me? I will *fucking* kill you."

He left the door open, staggering away from the van, catching his breath, leaving them to watch his feet kick up gravel dust as another plane roared overhead.

Focusing on the road ahead, the headlights passing by at speed, he felt stronger. He wouldn't let them know they'd transformed him—that they'd hardened his resolve like galvanized steel. He breathed fire. His rage was a jet engine. Without it, he would plummet to the Earth. He would crash and burn on the tarmac.

They had opened up his eyes.

He realized what he'd wanted all along, and now he knew how to get it.

He breathed.

He wouldn't turn back and thank them.

He *breathed*.

SHYLA REMAINED SILENT a moment, letting his words sink in. Her chest sagged suddenly with a gush of air, and she realized she'd been holding her breath for the last few minutes of Angel's story, as if in sympathy.

"That was you, wasn't it? The man in the story?"

Angel nodded.

Shyla considered her reply. "My mother always used to say, 'Hug your enemies, sugar. Make them into friends.' I always thought that was silly advice. If that had happened to me, I would have gotten them arrested. Did you call the cops?"

He shook his head, not wanting or not able to meet her eye.

"Why not?" She heard the anger in her tone, and told herself to dial it back. It wasn't an interrogation, not like what she'd faced after what had happened to her.

"I thought if I did it would only show them how much they'd hurt me. That they'd beaten me. It's amazing what we convince ourselves to avoid humiliation."

"But what if they did it again to someone else after you?" she asked, frustrated. "What if they *killed someone* the next time?"

"I guess that never occurred to me," he said. "I suppose I'd have to live with the guilt, if it did."

"Did they do *that* to you?" Shyla said, pointing at the long, faded scar down the side of his face.

At first Angel didn't seem to know what she meant. "Oh, this?" He drew a finger down the dark, jagged line. "No, that scar's from a long time ago. I don't even remember it happening."

An uncomfortable silence fell between them. She didn't want to tell him—she felt *compelled* to. He'd been violated. Not in the same way as she had when she was a teenager, but degradation and humiliation were difficult to quantify.

"I know how hard it is, when someone abuses you, to do what you have to do," Shyla said. "I know what it's like to feel helpless and still have to try and be strong."

"Oh?" he said.

She nodded. "When I was fifteen, I wasn't comfortable in my body. I was a sad girl. Didn't have many friends. This one day, an older boy, Donny Holbrook, asked me to go to the movies with him. I was so excited I didn't even think to wonder why he'd ask me, out of everyone he could have asked. Anyway, he told me to meet him behind the theater before the show. We were going to see the new *King Kong* movie. I didn't realize then that it was part of the joke."

The silence drew out as she gathered her thoughts, the dildo forgotten between them. The air conditioning unit hummed in the corner, blasting cool air that froze the sweat under her arms.

"I don't want to tell it," she said, "not in gory detail like you did. I came to terms with what happened a long time ago. I *had* to. Because of the way I was found. I only told the police because the guy who found me called them. I only told my father because the police made me. The more I talked about it, the less power it had over me." She sighed, her breath shaking from the rapid beat of her heart. "But I'm done telling it. The world doesn't need another rape story, you know? And it happened *so long* ago…"

"That doesn't invalidate it," Angel said. "There's no statute of limitations on pain."

Shyla frowned at that. "No, you're right. But those boys already faced their judgment for what they did to me. We were all just kids."

"Shall we take this out?" Angel said, indicating the dildo.

"No," she said, shaking her head. "I need to feel it."

Angel didn't look like he understood.

"I need to feel *whole*. For the part of me *they* took away."

He looked down at the black circle protruding from her rosy folds, and back up to her cold gaze.

"The short version is, Donny and his friends took turns raping me with a baseball bat in the woods behind the theater," Shyla said, hitching a breath. "The worst part about it, other than the pain and the shame of it, is that I should have known better. I *knew* I should have turned and left when I saw the other two boys with him. But I convinced myself to stay." She shook her head. "That I was being an idiot, it wouldn't be nice, I'd screwing things up with Donny, who was pretty and popular, and if I just played along everything would be okay. You should always listen to that voice when something doesn't feel right. Always look out for the red flags. Stop worrying about being nice, about making a scene. I know that now. I learned it the hard way that night."

"I'm sorry that happened to you, Shyla."

"Thank you. Before, when you asked about children, I've always wanted them," she said. "After what those boys did to me I'll never know that joy. And I think my mother would have been okay that I never hugged them."

"I'm sure she would have." He gave her a thin smile. "You've probably been asked this before, but have you thought about adoption? Who knows, you might strike gold and get someone like me," he added, giving her a wry smile.

"Someday, maybe. If I ended up with a kid anywhere near as considerate and intelligent as you, I'd count myself lucky."

They both smiled in the silence that followed. She wiped a tear from her cheek.

"One last story, then," Angel said. "And then we'll get down to business."

"I think I need to pee first," Shyla said. "Do you mind if I...?" She gestured toward the dildo.

Angel nodded. "Oh, absolutely."

Shyla thanked him, and grasped what was visible of the shiny black pylon. She noticed her pussy had left a little creaminess around the base of it, and wiped it away quickly before easing the dildo out of herself.

She'd be sore after this—hell, she was sore *now*— but she knew she'd get back into shape easily enough. It was mostly in the inner thighs where she felt it, the slightly sharp, hard rubber rim around the bottom leaving painful red lines on her flesh like the smother box had.

She pulled out the rest, feeling emptied as the tip came out of her with a sucking sound. Angel watched with wide eyes as her sticky opening contracted to its normal, discreet cleft.

"Did you know there's a world record for the widest vagina?" he asked.

"It doesn't surprise me."

"A Scottish giant named Anna Swan gave birth to a twenty-two pound boy in 1879. His head was nineteen centimeters. That's about six inches in diameter. You've just taken five and a half."

"Did I?" Off his nod, she said, "I'm not sure if I should be proud or concerned." She pushed herself out of bed with a restrained groan. She was limber, no way she would make much money in the business without being flexible, in so many ways. But being a large woman still had its disadvantages, one of which was rising from soft furniture like beds or sofas.

She walked barefoot to the bathroom, legs tingly with pins and needles, sashaying so Angel would get a good look at her ass. Not that he seemed to care. At first she'd thought he had a thing for big girls, but he didn't appear to have much interest in her body. Even when he was fucking her with the toys, he reminded her more of a gynecologist than a sex partner, aside from his hairdresser's chattiness. *What's he getting out of this?* she wondered. *Is this therapy for him?*

Have a quick pee, maybe stand in the shower for a rinse—*Try not to slip, don't want to suffer the same fate Mary*—and return refreshed for what she hoped would be a good, solid fuck from a hard, thick cock.

Passing Angel's bag of tricks, she took a peek inside. Aside from a fleshy, suction-cup dildo, there only appeared to be a checkered hand towel, a thing of hand sanitizer, and an unlabeled bottle that looked like it might contain peroxide or nail polish remover.

No red flags to worry about, as far as she could see.

MAN(NEQUIN)

SHYLA EMERGED FROM the bathroom a short time later doused in a thick miasma of sweet perfume. Her inner thighs glistened as if she'd rinsed herself off in the tub, and Angel was glad for that. Her sweat, during the brief story of her rape, had turned a tad sour. He watched her ease onto the bed and lay back against the headboard.

Angel knew he'd gained her sympathy with the story of his rebirthing in the back of a van. She wouldn't have told him what those boys had done to her if he hadn't. But if he wanted her to go along peacefully with what he planned, he'd have to make her *really* feel sorry for him. He'd have to tell her the one story he'd never told anyone, at least not all of it.

He'd have to tell her about Andy.

He'd have to tell her about the *mannequin*.

"I'm ready when you are," she said, getting comfortable.

He hoped she was comfortable, for what he had to say. Because what happened that night had meant he'd never been able to be comfortable again in his life. All that would change today, though.

"This story is the darkest one of all," Angel said.

"Goodie. Will there be a sex toy accompaniment?"

"Not for this one."

"Oh, poo," Shyla said with a pout.

"No poo in this one either, I'm afraid."

She laughed.

Angel joined her, glad for some levity between what she'd told him and the last story he had to tell. After this, they would get down to business.

He was ready.

He hoped Shyla was ready, too.

"This story is about a girl—"

WHO LOVED SOMETHING so much she was willing to do whatever it took to get it.

Bethany Chastain lived in a small bungalow on the East Side with her mother and their tabby cat Sniffles. Her mom was a kind of peculiar, artsy type—I'd heard some people call her a cat lady, but since the family only had one cat it didn't seem fair. Bethany was seventeen years old when she came to the Lonely Motel with her prom date, and because of her embarrassment over her mother's odd behavior, he was her first. Before then she'd always worried they would have to come over to her house at some point, and her mother would mortify her by acting the way she always did and scaring them away.

Everybody in the neighborhood knew Cora Chastain. The woman's conduct didn't just bother her daughter; Bethany saw that others were put-off by it as well, even *disgusted*. Cora Chastain didn't seem to get it, though. She had no idea how to interact with people. She was socially oblivious. See, Bethany's mom had been diagnosed in her teens with histrionic personality disorder, and because of it she was constantly seeking attention, especially from men. Delivery boys had it the hardest, scurrying back to their Volkswagen Rabbits when Bethany's mother answered the door in a frilly teddy, and they caught sight of her jailbait daughter peeking around the corner from the kitchen. It got so bad, restaurants refused to take her order. Turnaround for mail carriers in their area was the highest in the city.

See, Cora Chastain didn't just flirt. "Sexual harassment" was a better term. The few times Bethany did have boys over when she was younger, at a birthday party or to study with a group of friends, before she was old enough to realize not everyone's parents acted like her mother did, her mother competed with her for the boys' approval. She'd ruffle their hair, or pinch their cheeks and wink at them, and she'd always be wearing something low-cut, something tight. During one birthday party, she came up from her workshop all covered in splotches of wet clay like dried semen, sticking to the flimsy fabric of her tube top and hardened around her jutting nipples. And she was always, "*Such* a mess," even when she'd spent half an hour dolling herself up in front of the bathroom mirror.

Bethany grew up with weird ideas about sex because of this. Her mother had all but dry-hump a horrified Jehovah's Witness at the door (they'd avoided their house like the Plagues of Egypt passing over the homes of righteous Hebrews after that incident, the word spreading through their ranks down at the Kingdom Hall), and she'd heard her mother having sex with countless strange men who Cora would refer to as Bethany's "uncles." By her mother's count, Bethany had more uncles than picnics had ants.

Cora's tormented daughter slept in a small bedroom in their basement, and didn't much like it down there. It was dank and smelled like mildew. It was opposite the furnace, which ticked and hummed loudly at night. Too hot in the winter, too cold in the summer. Her mother had her workshop down there, which was always a mess, and Bethany would often be woken up by the sound of power tools.

Her mother did multimedia art, incorporating clay, found objects, woodworking, painting, and collages. Some of it was brilliant. She'd had a few gallery showings, but once word got out how difficult it was to work with her, be they men—whom she glommed onto—or women—who'd just about be challenged to pistols at dawn, her work was relegated to her own small booth at a local farmer's market. Even they refused to have her there, eventually.

Sometimes her mother's collection of crafts and supplies got so out of hand they'd spill over into Bethany's room, so for the longest time, she shared her bedroom with a store mannequin. The first few weeks, after her mother had stuffed him into a dark corner of her room the year she turned nine, Bethany would come in after school or from the bathroom, forget he was there, and freak out all over again.

Even worse than that was that her mother hadn't even bothered to *dress* him. His chiseled chest and the smooth Ken Doll lump between his legs, not quite anatomically correct, but enough to cause her to give it shy little glances, to make her think of men stepping out of the pool in tight bathing suits at the neighborhood Y, or the boys climbing rope in their red Adidas gym shorts. She considered putting clothes on him herself, but she knew her mother would accuse her of being "*so* puritanical," and make the whole situation a million times worse.

Over time, she got used to him, where even his nakedness didn't embarrass her anymore. She went so far as to give him a name: with his smooth bald head, his vacant blue eyes, and muscular body, she thought he looked like an Andy.

Bethany would come home after school, and with her mother at work, or upstairs with another long-lost uncle, she'd tell Andy about her day. At first she thought of it like how some girls wrote in their journals, *Dear Diary... etcetera etcetera*, treating it like a living entity who actually listened to their stories. Harmless enough, she thought. Like talking to Sniffles the cat.

Over time, Andy became her friend. He didn't

judge, like her girlfriends did. He didn't offer half-baked solutions and platitudes, like a boy might. He simply listened. He was her sounding board. Andy stood in stoic opposition to ideas she knew were silly, that she'd only spoken aloud to get them out of her head (ideas like killing her mother with poison, or leaving the back door open "accidentally" so Sniffles would wander off and stop getting his dandruff all over the couch cushions). Andy's crooked smile offered approval and sympathy as required.

Bethany had her first period at the early age of eleven. Her mother had paraded her proudly around the house, cheering for her when they went to buy maxi-pads—"My little girl's a *woman* now!" she told a bemused clerk behind the pharmacy counter, shaking Bethany's fist like she'd won a gold medal for high diving—and promptly driving her to her own gynecologist to get a prescription for The Pill. "I won't have my baby having babies," she told the startled doctor, who looked a bit like Mr. Weatherbee from the *Archie* comics, while her daughter sat red-faced, her eyes rolling back in her head in complete and utter embarrassment.

Around that time Bethany decided she'd better practice kissing boys if she was going to start going to dances and dating like the other girls in school. Andy's crooked smile seemed to express he was more than happy to oblige.

She locked her bedroom door, and turned on the radio to the classic rock station she enjoyed. While

John Cougar sang a little ditty about two American kids named Jack and Diane, Bethany approached her mannequin friend with a shy smile, knowing that if her mother caught her it would be absolutely mortifying. Cora Chastain would probably brag to the pizza delivery kid about her daughter's "sexual awakening" and/or "exploration."

Andy was a foot taller, so Bethany had to stand up on her tiptoes. His blue eyes peered over her head as she planted a kiss on his smooth plastic lips, the way she'd kiss Sniffles when the cat didn't have too much dry skin in his fur.

It didn't... feel quite right. It was cold, for one thing. And dry. She didn't know what sort of reaction she was expecting, but it wasn't exactly *electrifying*.

Feet back on the floor, she looked up into Andy's blank stare, mirroring her disappointment. Her gaze fell on his smooth pubis. She remembered her mother rubbing her crotch on the leg of another "uncle" at the dinner table one night, the way Sniffles sometimes humped pillows when he was In Heat. She couldn't reach to mimic the action, not without getting up on a chair and risking tipping Andy over, sending the both of them sprawling to the floor, so she crouched down and hugged Andy around the knees. He was heavier than she'd imagined, and he almost fell over backwards, but she managed to keep him upright, her nose pressed against his crotch, and with a strained grunt she threw him down on her bed.

Andy's arms didn't bend at the elbow or wrist,

just at the shoulders—that was one problem she noticed right away. They were posed in what she thought of as a slightly effeminate way, one hand up with the elbow cocked at his waist, not clenched or flat but half-open, as if her were holding a purse. The other only slightly bent, the hand just sort of… limp.

She pushed him over to one side of the bed, his head on the pillow, and laid down beside him. Even side by side it felt awkward. She couldn't pretend they were husband and wife with Andy staring at the ceiling. She pushed his left arm down and climbed on top of him, sitting on his stomach at first, then sliding down to the lump at his crotch. She placed one hand on his chest, and the other so that his right hand almost seemed to hold her by the arm. Bethany looked deep into those vacant blue eyes, lowered her face to him, and pressed her lips against his.

On the radio the traffic report gave way to Foreigner's "I Want to Know What Love Is," the ultimate slow dance song. Reaching out with her left hand, she slipped it behind Andy's head. She stuck out her tongue, the way they did in the movies, opening and closing her moistened lips like a fish in a tank.

When she began grinding against Andy's bump, a steady, rhythmic warmth arose from her vagina and spread throughout her whole body, seemingly pulsating along with the music. Her kisses grew frantic as she slipped a hand behind his head, rubbing herself harder and faster against his pelvis, the poly-cotton blend of her panties moving *contretemps* to her thrusts, doubling the sensation. She grasped his smooth buttocks. She stroked his bald head. She darted her tongue in and out, pushing it against his slightly parted lips.

With the music turned up so high, she allowed herself a small moan, and that was when it finally happened. After what seemed like minutes of shuddering, panting, and squeaking moans, Bethany rolled off of Andy and lay her hot, sweaty head against the pillow.

Although she didn't know it then, Bethany had experienced her first orgasm, with a dummy.

The next day when Bethany came home from school, she dropped her books on the dresser and carried Andy over to her bed. The following day, she did it—whatever *it* was—two times, and fell asleep with Andy at her side.

She carried on like that for months before her mother took Andy away from her, and it wasn't what you might think. She hadn't caught her daughter doing what she called her "dance" with Andy. What happened was that Bethany came home one day to find Andy disassembled, his parts nailed or glued to a sheet of old, rotting plywood. Cora had strung up barbed wire through his jumbled parts, and glued photographs from magazines in the spaces between, candid shots of Jared Leto, Rob Lowe, Patrick Swayze and others. Painted above this jumbled mess she would undoubtedly call "art" was the strange word

PHALLUCIDE in dripping blood red letters.

Cora herself stood in front of it, covered in plaster and paint, blasting Andy's crotch smoother with the belt sander. When she saw her daughter standing with her mouth agape at the foot of the stairs, she flipped up her safety goggles.

"Tada!" she said. "Well, what do you think, hon?"

Bethany bolted to her room so her mother wouldn't see her cry.

"Is it really that bad?" Cora shouted after her.

Weeping into Andy's pillow, Bethany imagined she could still smell the sharp cologne of his pungent plastic skin. Long after her mother went to bed, she crept out of her room and stood in front of her beloved. She ran her fingers over the jagged edges where her mother had torn her heart to pieces.

Their strange love was over.

One night she came home from school to find the whole thing gone. Her mother told her the piece sold to a gallery owner in Bridgeport. Just as she had feared, Bethany would never see him again.

Eventually she got over the initial trauma of losing Andy, but just seeing a department store mannequin brought it all flooding back again, and sometimes she would have to lock herself inside the change room just to hide her tears.

Beth was seventeen when she had her first date with a real boy. We were in a few of the same classes together, English and Psychology. Another one, too—I can't recall. We both swam regularly, me on the team and Beth at the Y, and we hit it off pretty quickly. She was the first person I remember, outside of the kids at the foster home, who didn't feel sorry for me because I was an orphan. I suppose because she'd never known her father she understood what it was like. The fact that she hated her mother probably didn't hurt, either.

I had my own place by the time we met. If you remember from the last story, I'd lived with my foster family until I was sixteen, that's when I moved out on my own for reasons I won't get into now, but still continued at school. I worked evenings and weekends at a restaurant, starting as a dishwasher and moving my way up to line cook by the time I graduated. It gave me enough money to get out of the foster home, which had become a pretty poisonous environment, and move into a room with a kitchen and bathroom I shared with UB students and low-income singles.

Beth and I started seeing each other in the first semester of twelfth grade. I didn't meet her mother until the night of the prom. When we weren't going to the movies, or getting ice cream and doing other things normal kids did, we spent a lot of our time at my place. By the time prom came around, I was pretty sure I loved her. One of the things I respected about her was that she never pressured me for sex. Considering my background, I appreciated that. There were others who *did*—one of the reasons I had to leave the foster home. Still, we made out quite a bit, along with occasional dry humping, which in retrospect—after she told me the Andy Story—made a lot of sense.

On Prom Night, that all changed. Bethany wanted sex, and she'd made it pretty clear when she told me some of the other kids were going to be staying at the Lonely Motel, and that I should rent us a room.

See, I grew up terrified of sex. "Scared shitless" is a better term. I knew what sex led to—STDs were the least of my worries. You know, I'd hear stories about condoms breaking, women not taking their pill, that sort of thing, and I'd think, *Knowing my luck it'll be that first time and I'll be stuck with a kid the rest of my life. Won't be able to give it up because of how fucked up that made me. Won't be able to raise it because I had no parents for role models…*

So I made a conscious decision to avoid sex, even when two of the girls at my foster home—the social worker would call them my foster sisters, though we never thought of each other as "family" the way real families do—and a handful of girls at school were making concerted efforts to get me into bed with them. With Beth, I decided to make a go of it, since we loved each other. Or so I thought.

Being on the swim team, I knew all the techniques to make myself faster, to hold my breath longer. It helps to be tall and slim if you want to be a great swimmer. Sleek. So all the guys on the team, we had to get rid of all the hair on our arms, chests and legs, to move faster through the water. Some of the guys shaved because they couldn't take the pain, but Charlie and I waxed. The football team would make fun of us, call us fags and ask where we bought our pantyhose, because "only women wax," but a lot of the girls seemed to like it. Charlie got laid constantly, which probably solidified his decision to get into the porn business after high school, since he broke his shoulder in senior year and had to quit the team.

I started shaving my head that year, too. I was balding prematurely, and the scar messed with my hairline anyway, so it just made sense.

All of this made me the perfect man for Beth Chastain, but I didn't know it then.

So I drove out to the Lonely Motel in my little shitbox Toyota, and paid the desk clerk for a room for the night. He was an older gentleman wearing pressed slacks and a brown shirt with a wide '70s collar, his gray comb-over slicked back with the same pungent hair tonic he used on his nicotine-stained mustache.

"Lucky you," he said as he put my cash in the till. "Got yourself the last room in the house."

He handed me the key to Room 6, which I stuffed into the pants pocket of my rented tux without much thought, having no idea of its significance until much later.

When I picked up Beth, her mother was so elated for her daughter she forgot about herself for the moment and didn't try to hit on me. Beth had told me all of her horror stories—aside from the Andy Story, which she would tell me later that night—so we'd both been expecting her mom to throw herself on me in an attempt to steal me away. Instead she was polite, dressed modestly—for Cora Chastain, modest was a tight-fitting sweater that didn't reveal too much cleavage—and she snapped photos as Beth came downstairs in her dress—she was gorgeous, by the way—a couple of me putting Beth's corsage on her wrist, and several of the two of us out on the front lawn.

Beth brought her school backpack with her for the overnight stay. It felt like she'd packed a brick in there as I lugged it to my car, and I said so. She practically tore it off my shoulder, as if she was worried I'd go snooping inside of it, and tucked it into the backseat herself.

The drive to prom was pretty awkward. She kept stealing small glances at me, and I kept missing her eyes as she'd turn away. We laughed nervously about her mother's surprisingly normal behavior, and speculated about what sort of shenanigans Charlie would get up to with his two dates. All the while the specter of what we'd planned to do once the dance let out hung over our heads.

If only we'd both been nervous about the same thing.

Once we got to school the atmosphere lightened a bit. We relaxed. Charlie was such a clown in his pink tux, with a date on each arm. Our laughter came easier. We drank the punch Charlie had spiked with a bottle of Fleischmann's vodka his older brother bought. We danced.

We were up there dancing to "You Oughta Know" when the inevitable slow dance hit. Somebody whose name I didn't hear over the loud revelry between songs had requested "I Want to Know What Love Is." It could have been Beth herself, I suppose. I didn't know the song's significance, but I saw the way her eyes lit up when the song came on, so I pulled her close and we spun around and around, and when I raised her chin to look into her eyes, I saw that she'd been crying.

I kissed her right there on the dance floor. A couple of the guys wolf whistled, and Charlie applauded.

On the drive to the Lonely Motel, Beth said she had something to share. She didn't want to tell me. It embarrassed her. But she "thought it was only fair," as she put it, and so she told me about her mannequin. Not the whole story—the finer details came later, when I visited her in prison. A CliffsNotes version, I guess you might say.

When she was finished we'd already pulled up out front of our room for the night. She was looking at me, clearly expecting a horrified reaction. "I'll understand if you never want to see me again," she said. I loved her so much in that moment, her vulnerability, the fact that she'd felt comfortable enough to open up about something so obviously shameful—not to mention *painful*—to her. I kissed her.

"I hope that was better than Andy," I said when our lips parted, hoping it wouldn't offend or embarrass her further.

Beth giggled and nodded. "I love you, Johnny," she said to me.

"JOHNNY? *YOU'RE* JOHNNY?"

"I didn't mean to reveal that yet," Angel said, although he'd told his story exactly as planned. "Now you know why this room is so important to me."

"Jenny and Johnny… that was you, too." Shyla had sat up abruptly at the sound of his real name, and now she was putting things together, playing catch-up.

"The things that happened in this room," Angel said, "I'll remember for the rest of this life."

"Wait a minute. You said 'when I visited her in prison.' What did Beth do, Angel? Or should I call you *Johnny*?"

"You can call me Jonah for all it matters," he said. "In here I'm Angel, because I should have been dead. What Beth did to me is why we're here, you and I. It's the reason I began to connect the dots, like you're doing now. There are things I need to… *unburden* myself of… and then, with any luck, I'll be ready to begin again."

Shyla tried to parse his words, but they seemed illusive, just out of her reach. She said, "Okay, then.

Angel, Johnny—" She shook her head in confusion. "—*whatever* your name is: finish your story."

He did.

I LOVED BETH, and I thought she loved me. But the truth was she could never love anyone, because her love died the day her mother cut him to pieces and stuck them onto a slab of old plywood.

We walked hand-in-hand to Room 6, me lugging Beth's backpack on one shoulder the way kids used to, and Beth holding her heels. At the stoop I let go of her hand to get the keys from my pocket—for a second there I thought I'd lost them, that they'd slipped through a hole in the pants or fallen out while we were dancing, and the relief was profound when my fingers grasped the worn vermillion key fob.

I could almost hear the room sigh as I opened the door.

Some part of me thought it would be fun if I carried Beth over the threshold, like new husbands did for their brides on their honeymoon. So I dropped her bag at the door and hoisted her up, and very gently laid her down on the bed, the way she'd brought Andy to her bed countless times when she was a little girl.

Beth laid her head on the pillow, looking up at me with dazzlingly bright green eyes. I wanted her so badly right then that all of my fears, all of my worries, *everything* just disappeared, and I kissed her.

I should have been concerned when she rose up

from the pillow and pushed me over onto my back, but by then I was so in the moment, every part of me wanting to be all over every part of her, like lead shavings on a magnet, that it really didn't hit me. She straddled me, the way she'd done in my bedroom and on my sofa a dozen times or more, making my cock so hard my underwear would be sticky with pre-cum by the time she'd roll off me, exhausted, onto her back.

But now it was *real*. Now we were going to Do It.

I didn't understand until much later it was all a part of her fantasy. That when we were making out, I was never Johnny—I wasn't even *Angel*. With my smooth chest and my bald head, I was only ever the mannequin to her.

I was *Andy*.

In the next room, some kids were playing The Pixies at full volume. "Wave of Mutilation" gave way to "Debaser," so they must have had the CD player on shuffle. In the silence between songs, Beth tore her lips from mine and whispered, "I've got a surprise for you," into my ear.

She hopped off me, and went to the door, where I'd left her bag. First she flicked off the overhead lights, and I flicked on the dim bedside lamp so she could see to heft her backpack to the bathroom. She blew me a kiss as she walked past the foot of the bed.

The Boy Scouts tell you, "Be Prepared." That's the Scout's Motto. Prepared in mind, prepared in body, and I was definitely prepared in that department. My hard-on throbbed so much I hoped I wasn't staining the inside of my rented pants. Eagerly, I stripped down to my underwear, and tore the condom out of my wallet—I know you're not supposed to keep them there, but that wasn't common knowledge back then. A lot of guys I knew had condoms in their wallets so long they left rings in the leather.

The bathroom door opened and for a moment Beth stood silhouetted by its pale yellow light. She'd put on a see-through baby blue babydoll which clung to her curves. I'd never seen so much of her before, we'd always been fully clothed, aside from the few times we'd gone swimming at the Y together where she'd worn a one-piece swimsuit. A cloud of perfume hung around her as she moved lithely toward the bed, barely masking a sharper smell beneath it. As she climbed on top of me, the cool sensation of wet fabric on my skin came as a pleasant surprise as she slicked the underside of my shaft with her panties— I'd expected her to be warm. She rose again after two quick thrusts, and I thought she might slip out of her oddly cold underwear then, but instead she pushed her sopping wet pussy down over my nose and mouth.

Before I had a chance to consider holding my breath my lungs had filled with the unpleasantly sweet chemical smell she'd used to soak her panties. I tried to throw her off me, but she had my head locked between her strong swimmer's thighs, and with every breath my muscles were getting more numb and harder to control.

"I love you, my angel," she said, and the music faded away, and then I was out.

I've pieced together what happened next from the police report, and from what Bethany told me much later from prison. For a long time I couldn't think about what happened to me that night without suffering a complete mental collapse. It was just too much to comprehend. That someone who seemed so nice and caring could have done what she did—it was impossible to believe. But it happened. I've had to look at the evidence of what she did to me every day since.

When I came to it was because of the sound, not the pain. In fact, there wasn't much pain at all, just a sort of dull ache, I suppose because of the chloroform she'd used on me. Back when they used to use chloroform for anesthetics, you had to be careful. Too much and you could kill the patient. Too little, and they'd wake up mid-procedure.

I woke up to a high-pitched whine. I was numb from the neck down, and it was raining on my face. Barely audible above the buzzing, The Pixies sang "Here Comes Your Man." Beth was crouched over me with a look of fixed concentration. I thought I must be hallucinating, because her arms and babydoll were the same color as the carpet in the dim light, and warm rain kept pattering against my cheeks and forehead even though we were inside.

I managed to raise my head just enough to see

what was making all the noise.

Her mother's belt sander spun, tearing the meat and flesh of my scrotum and flaccid penis to shreds under the whirring motor. A wet flap of skin splattered against my throat, and that's when I became unhinged. I screamed.

Beth looked up at me not with sympathy but with genuine anger. I was supposed to be unconscious. I'd spoiled her half-baked plan to turn me into a mannequin, to make me smooth all over the way *he* was, her beloved—her Andy. She pressed down harder in response, the sandpaper obliterating the fatty tissue above my cock—

"JESUS... JESUS *CHRIST*, Angel," Shyla said, her face as pale as the sheets. "I'm so sorry."

Angel continued unabated. "If someone hadn't chosen that exact moment to plug something in and blow the power," he said, "I probably would have died of blood loss. But someone did, and the room went dark, and everything was silent except for me, screaming at the top of my lungs.

"Beth turned off the sander to shush me. 'Be quiet, Andy, you'll get me in trouble!' she yelled into my face, but I wasn't Andy and I wouldn't be quiet, and when she tried to cover my mouth I bit her hand and screamed ten times louder.

"A second later the door swung open and rebounded against the interior wall. The desk clerk shouted, 'Jesus *fuck*!' The light from the parking lot was just bright enough for him to see Beth's handiwork.

"I'd never been so glad to see someone in my life. He'd never been so sorry to see something in his. Or maybe he had, the day he found Mary Booker and her unborn baby in the bathtub. A baby boy the hospital named John."

Shyla said nothing, stunned silent as Angel kept telling his story.

"I blacked out again after that," he said. "When I woke the second time, I was in the hospital, my entire pelvis bandaged. The pain was gigantic, an Everest of pain. I just wanted to be unconscious again. I wished I'd let Beth finish the job. I wished I'd shut up and let her kill me.

"A team of surgeons told me they could fix my urethra so I could urinate without a catheter, but I'd never be able to have sex without genital reconstruction, and I'd never be able to have children outside of in vitro. Not that I wanted children," Angel added. "I wouldn't know how to raise one if I had."

A tear rolled down Shyla's cheek. She hitched in a shaky breath.

"No one came to visit me," he said, "not even Chuck. I didn't blame him. After what she did, how could he look at me? I'd been mutilated. She'd erased my manhood. I was sexless. Neutered. A mannequin man. That's what the papers called me, when Beth told her story to the police, and I wasn't even a man yet. *The Mannequin Man.* I was just glad they couldn't name me because I was a minor. But everyone at school knew. They *pitied* me. I could see it in their eyes."

"What did you *do*? How could you go on after something like that?"

"I did what I had to. I survived. Just like I did when my mother died in the tub." He traced the scar on his face with a finger, the scar made by his mother's coat hook. "With one more scar to add to the collection."

"That was you, too," she said. "Mary's boy."

Angel bent for his backpack. He found the slip of old paper, torn out of the book of Lonely Motel stationary in December of 1980, and let it fall gently onto Shyla's lap. She picked it up and read the words aloud, "'To my unborn child'... Oh God, Angel. I can't. I can't read this."

"Would you like to see what Bethany did to me?"

Shyla shook her head. "No, I don't—I *can't*..."

Angel stood, and began to unzip his pants.

"*Please*," she said.

He stepped out of his pants and slid down the boxers.

(STILL)BORN AGAIN

ANGEL STOOD NAKED before her. Hard pink scar tissue covered his groin from his navel to his inner thighs. In the middle of this a small nub of flesh protruded, about the size of a thumb knuckle, with a slit down the middle so he could urinate.

Shyla refused to look, covering her eyes with her hands.

"Look at me, Shyla," he said. "I'm *paying* you to look at me."

She wouldn't.

"*Look at me*, goddammit!"

Hesitantly her hands fell from her eyes and she turned to him. She wouldn't look down, like someone trying desperately not to peek at a woman's cleavage.

"Look at what she did to me," Angel said.

She looked. Her eyes widened for a brief moment before she covered them again, breathing, "Oh, God," through her teeth.

"Have you ever thought," Angel said, pulling up his boxers, concealing his ultimate shame, "have you ever thought your life would be better off if you could start over again? Like a weset button?"

Shyla nodded behind her hands.

"You can uncover your eyes now," he told her, zipping up his fly.

She lowered her hands. The relief in her tear-streaked eyes amused him, but he didn't show it.

"See, I've tried weligion. I've tried meditation. I've tried therapy and webirthing. I've even tried love. But none of these took away my pain. It's always been there, since I was born. My mother was w-raped. My father," he sneered, "a *rapist*. I'll never be able to undo what Beth did to me, but I can start over. I know I can. I've started to pwactice holding my bweath again."

"Why did you call me here?" Shyla said, her lower lip quivering. "To tell me your stories? To make me feel sorry for you? I do feel sorry for you, Angel, I *do—*"

"*I don't want your pity!*" Angel yelled. Shyla flinched as drops of spit struck her face. "I want your cunt," he said calmly. "Your magnificent, wonderfully large cunt. See, I learned a lot from Bethany. I learned that if you want something badly enough, you have to do what it takes to get it. No matter the cost."

Her tearful eyes met his. "What is it you *want*? You want to rape me? You want to—what? Put things inside me again?"

"Not *things*, Shyla. *Me*."

"You...?"

He could tell from her eyes she didn't understand, that he would have to make himself absolutely clear. "I want you to accept me," he said.

"I do accept you, Angel. Johnny. I *do*, I just—"

"You said you need to feel full. I can give you that, Shyla. I can. But I need something from you. That's what you called a 'mutually beneficial transaction,' wouldn't you say? I'd like for it to be consensual," he added, in a tone implying he would take what he wanted if she wouldn't give it to him willingly. "I want you to accept this *miwacle* I have to give you."

"Miracle? *What are you talking about?*" she cried, her breasts heaving.

"I'm going to give you the opportunity to give birth," he said.

"Birth? What the fuck are you—?"

"To *me*, Shyla. I'm going to squeeze my head into your vagina, and you're going to birth me."

She looked at his smooth bald scalp. "*No…*" she whispered, shaking her head so violently her chin waggled.

"I'm very sorry to hear that," Angel said, and bent to reach into his backpack. In one quick, practiced movement, he unsnapped the cap off the bottle and squirted chloroform into the hand towel. When he rose again, Shyla was pushing herself out of bed, taking quick, panicky breaths. He strode toward her and caught her as she got to her feet, jumping onto her back and reaching over her smooth shoulders to smother her with the chloroformed rag.

She swung herself back and forth, trying to shake him from her back like an animal shaking off fleas.

He kept the pressure steady over her mouth and nose, wrapping his long legs tightly around her thighs. Eventually her arms stopped swinging. She stumbled forward, her head struck the door, and she fell sideways. Angel leapt to his feet as she landed on the floor with a solid thump, unconscious.

He knelt down beside her. Checked her throat and then her wrist for a pulse. It was slow but steady. She'd live.

Angel grabbed her by the wrists and dragged her back to the bed. She was too heavy to lift onto the mattress. He supposed he should have known it might come to this, and have been deadlifting to strengthen his core muscles.

It didn't matter. The floor would do.

He rolled her onto her back, spread her legs, and raised her dress. Her eyes fluttered behind the lids. Angel crossed to the dresser and took off his clothes, folding them in front of the mirror. He pumped out a handful of Slippin' Slide, and slathered it onto his scalp and over his face until his whole head gleamed under the overhead lights. He pumped out a second handful, squishing it between his fingers where it dripped onto the vermillion carpet, leaving wet stains that looked like blood.

Returning to where Shyla lay, he found her snoring lightly, as if she'd just laid down for a nap. He knelt between her legs. Fear has sharpened her sweat, giving it a sour tang. He raised her left leg, pushing it aside to make room for his shoulder. The handful of lubricant moistened her vagina and inner thighs. He laid back between her legs, facing upward as if her were trying to look up her skirt, and rubbed the top of his smooth, wet head against her labia majora, the way Juicy had rubbed his cock up and down on Candy Rain's asshole.

Then he began to push.

He thought of Victor and Raylene and Irv, coaxing him on like a reluctant mother as they smothered him to death under their dirty old rug— and he pushed.

He thought of Jenny, who had loved him despite his handicap, who had started shooting heroin because he could only give her orgasms when she rode him, but he could never please her the way she'd wanted to be pleased with his tiny, mangled penis. He thought of her cold, dead vagina as he reached into her over and over again, removing bag after bag of the drug she had cast him aside for, the drug that had eventually killed her.

He pushed.

He thought of the Smother Man, and the dedication it must have taken to handcraft his smother box, and how he'd been born again under the weight of Shyla's cunt.

He pushed, and thought of Mary, his mother, her leg up on the rim of the bathtub, and the determination it must have taken to push a bent wire hanger into her womb to tear him out of her.

He *pushed*, and Shyla's lips parted, and he felt her

(121)

warmth swallow the top of his head, like how he'd felt the cool air on his scalp when he'd finally pushed free of the rug, their makeshift womb in the back of their van, and he pushed again, hearing her flesh tear.

He was in up to his eyebrows now, and even more determined to continue. This was the farthest he'd ever come. The other women hadn't even been able to take the narrow half of the dildo, and the ones who could had bored of his stories and left without his money.

Shyla and her perfectly flawed vagina were a godsend. She was damaged, like him. They were pieces of a larger cosmic puzzle. He was certain he would fit.

The top of his ears folded over. With another push, her vaginal opening forced his eyes closed, and he was enveloped in warm, wet darkness.

His nose would be the true test. He wormed his shoulders closer to her, edging toward her on the carpet, glad that he'd thought to make room by pushing up her legs. He performed a few preparatory breaths, and sucked in a huge lungful of air, hoping this next push would be the last.

He thrust his whole weight toward her.

The bridge of his nose cracked, shooting splintering pain directly into his eyeballs. The pain didn't trouble him. He'd been through much more agony in one breath than most people would feel in their entire lifetimes. Tasting blood, his own or hers, he had no idea, Angel pushed one last time, and her

(122)

pussy devoured his mouth, and his chin slipped inside of her throbbing organ.

Flesh covered every inch of his head, pulled taut over his face like a hot, wet balaclava. Her heartbeat thrummed in his ears. Her stomach juices gurgled like thunder in the darkness. Her insides shut out the chatter, the anger, the fear, the self-doubt. Her womb smothered his pain.

He'd done it.

Peace. At long last.

With an inward cheer, he prepared to make his escape. Goodbye Johnny. Goodbye Andy. Goodbye Mannequin Man. It was time to be *reborn*.

He would emerge from her an *Angel*.

A vivid image struck with sudden intensity, the tranquility of his new mother's womb penetrated by a sharp wire hanger tearing through his cheek. She was aborting him. She wanted him *removed*. Angel struggled, kicking out at the empty air in the musty room outside of her, whatever this vessel, this luggage, wanted to call herself. He knew he wasn't a fetus. He knew what he'd felt and seen wasn't happening now—it was a false memory of a moment too early in his previous life to have been remembered. It was a recurring nightmare… but he couldn't shake the feeling something was terribly wrong.

He had to get out. *Now.*

He pulled.

Muscular flesh held his chin firmly in place. He

couldn't move. He was stuck. Stuck inside an unconscious prostitute's vagina. Stuck, without even the room to exhale.

Angel's thoughts turned to Jonah, trapped for three days and three nights in the belly of the whale, and wondered if he prayed would God command Shyla to push him out of her. He couldn't hope for that, not with his lungs already tightening from lack of breath.

No. He was a survivor.

Struggling madly, he reached out for something to hold on to, until finally his fingers grasped Shyla's fleshy inner thighs. He pushed with his hands, simultaneously trying to pull his head free.

No movement. His chin held him firmly in place. *Breeched.*

He tried turning his head, hoping it would dislodge him, hoping he could pry himself from his sticky, smothering tomb by twisting his head back and forth, like loosening a bolt, like pulling out a fist, like removing a coat hanger—

What if I was always meant to die here? In this room? What if that's why I kept coming back—kept being pulled back, as if by some giant cosmic coat hanger—only surviving by the skin of my teeth—or the skin of my nuts?

He saw the headline: *Mannequin Man Dies in Bizarre Sex Act.*

He pondered fate. Choices. How sometimes things seemed to shift into place like a planetary alignment or a slot machine jackpot, and how the house almost always won.

Let me out, you fat bitch!

As the last breath escaped him, his wordless scream was lost to her flesh.

SHYLA AWOKE WITH an uncomfortable pressure against her internal organs. In the fuzziness of swimming up from oblivion, she imagined she was pregnant. *A baby! When? How?*

Immense joy washed over her, like waking from a dream in which the people she loved were no longer dead, and she could talk to her mother again the way they used to before the accident, and her father would look at her with love again instead of pity.

Then the memory resurfaced of Donny Holbrook, his two friends, and the baseball bat, and she knew it was all in her imagination.

Something *was* inside her, though. A dildo? The one Angel had used on her, the one that looked like a witch's hat?

Johnny, she corrected herself, *Johnny's dildo*, and the thought of his birth name reminded her of the ruptured bags of heroin, of the belt sander and his mangled member, of the rug and the coat hanger, and suddenly everything he'd told her that afternoon came flooding back like a gush of amniotic fluid, and she moaned.

Shyla raised herself up onto her elbows, grunting against the pain in her insides.

"*Oh no,*" she said, looking over the folds of her stomach at the purple arms, legs, and torso sticking out of her like a real-life human centipede. Blood had spilled onto his chest—whether it was hers or his she didn't know, but it was obvious from the burning pain down there that he'd torn her open. If she did make it out of here alive, she'd have to go through surgery again.

Is he dead? She couldn't tell. His arms hung limply over her legs, and he wasn't moving. She stared at his chest for a long moment, waiting for a breath—but nothing came.

On her own then. No forceps or belts to help her deliver this corpse back into the world. This *stillborn.*

She heaved, pressing down on her belly with both hands, pushing harder than she'd ever done in her life, difficult bowel movements notwithstanding.

He's not gonna come out...

Chin against chest. *Concentrate.* Her well-developed PC muscle strained against his lube-slicked head. She felt him begin to ooze out of her. *Push.* Eyes staring unfocused at the wood-paneled wall, at the painting of Jonah escaping the whale.

She reached for his shoulders, but her stomach got in the way. Groaning, she stretched her arms, wriggling her fingers, and the tips of her acrylic nails brushed uselessly against his skin.

Have to get to the phone. If I can make it...

A deep breath in through the nose, out through the teeth, and another hard push. Face red, pulse throbbing in her temples, her whole body pressed against the thing inside of her. Suddenly feeling enormous sympathy for that Scottish giantess, the one Angel had mentioned, whose vagina had won the Guinness Record.

Sweat beading her brow. *Focus.*

Quick, small breaths. *You can do it.*

Steeling against the pain.

PUSH, mama!

The tear in her vagina widened with fresh agony as Angel's head spilled out of her, thudding dully on the carpet. Shyla fell back in a pool of her own sweat and blood, exhausted and in pain, allowing herself to recover, waiting for the agony to subside before turning her attention to the dead man on the floor.

She watched him until his chest began to move on its own, a slow breath dragged through his gaping mouth. He was alive, at least. She allowed herself a sigh of relief, then rolled over onto her stomach and got to her knees.

Angel—*Johnny*—stared up at the ceiling, his face crusted by a mucousy film, the eyes glazed over, his mouth hung open, glistening with a runner of drool that spilled down his cheek and pattered onto the carpet. She slapped him. He flinched, but otherwise didn't react. Was he comatose? *Braindead?* In a vegetative state? She didn't know.

She was glad he'd survived. It meant she wouldn't have to explain anything to the police. She wouldn't have his death on her conscience either, even though he'd drugged her and—*somehow*—forced his entire head inside of her. It was impossible to believe, even after what she'd just experienced, but it was true. He'd *raped* her. Raped her with his head.

Still, a small part of her felt sorry for him, despite everything he'd done to merit her fury—the part of her that still wanted to believe everyone was capable of good, even monsters. The little girl who listened intently as her mother said, "Hug your enemies, sugar," when she came home crying after being picked on at school.

After all the pain he'd lived through, she still believed he deserved her pity.

I'm too nice, she thought. *Anyone else would just smother him with a fucking pillow.*

"I don't hate you," she said, as much to convince herself than to inform him. "Johnny? I don't hate you. I don't. I *pity* you."

Angel shifted where he lay, drawing his knees up to his chest.

"I don't know if you can hear me. I hope you can."

Curled into the fetal position, Angel blinked.

"Johnny? I'm going to nurse you back to health. Okay?"

His Adam's apple bobbed as he swallowed.

"I'll... I'll feed you. I'll change you. I'll bathe you."

Shyla scooped him up under his arms, and cradled him to her bosom. He looked so peaceful. She wondered where he was, in his mind. She wondered if he was at peace.

"You're going to stay right here until you get better," she promised him, hugging him to her. "Right here in this room."

A small sound escaped his lips, and she shushed him, patting his back as she rocked him gently in her arms.

~

ABOUT THE AUTHOR

 Duncan Ralston was born in Toronto and spent his teens in small-town Canada. As a "grownup," Duncan lives with his partner and their dog in Toronto, where he writes dark fiction about the things that disturb him. In addition to his twisted short stories found in *GRISTLE & BONE* and *VIDEO NASTIES*, the anthologies *EASTER EGGS & BUNNY BOILERS*, *WHAT GOES AROUND*, *DEATH BY CHOCOLATE*, *FLASH FEAR*, and the charity anthologies *DARK DESIGNS, BAH! HUMBUG!*, *VS: US vs UK HORROR*, and *THE BLACK ROOM MANUSCRIPTS Vol. 1*, he is the author of the novel *SALVAGE*, and the novellas *WILDFIRE*, *WHERE THE MONSTERS LIVE*, *WOOM*, and *THE METHOD* from Kindle Press.

For more delicious dark fiction, visit
www.DuncanRalston.com and
www.ShadowWorkPublishing.com.